TE DUE

| AUG 4 '69 | | | |
|---|---|---|---|
| MAY 28 '70 | | | |
| MAY 1 5 1970 | | | |
| | | | |
| | | | |
| | | | |
| | | | |
| | | | |
| | | | |
| | | | |
| | | | |
| | | | |
| | | | |
| | | | |
| | | | |
| | | | |
| | | | |
| GAYLORD | | | PRINTED IN U.S.A. |

# TOLD UNDER THE MAGIC UMBRELLA

# TOLD
# UNDER THE
# MAGIC UMBRELLA

Modern Fanciful Stories for
Young Children

*Selected by the*

LITERATURE COMMITTEE OF THE
ASSOCIATION FOR CHILDHOOD EDUCATION

Illustrated by
ELIZABETH ORTON JONES

NEW YORK
*THE MACMILLAN COMPANY*
1940

J
398
A

# TOLD UNDER THE MAGIC UMBRELLA

TO
THE CHILDREN
WHO LOVE
WONDER, MAGIC AND FUN

# FOREWORD

MAKE-BELIEVE is a great resource of childhood. It is
a child's first essay in imagination, his attempt to inter-
pret a strange and confusing world in terms of his own
understanding and to his own liking. Explanations of
the older mind are not always satisfactory; they take too
much for granted, and the child mind, insatiably curi-
ous, often prefers to invent its own explanations. Young
children are apt to have rather tidy minds; they dislike
loose ends instinctively; they want to find a reason for
everything, and where a reason is not forthcoming they
will promptly make one up for themselves, and more
often than not their reasoning takes the form of a story.
In a word, they are born creators of folklore, a folklore
entirely their own and concerned with the familiar
things around them.

The modern fairy tale—or fanciful tale, to make a
useful distinction—takes full account of this creative
instinct. It differs from its long line of predecessors in
concerning itself not so much with fantastic elements
outside the child's experience as with the more every-
day things of his own world. It realizes that magic, like
charity, begins best at home.

In this kind of story the child is not only audience,
he feels himself almost collaborator. At a certain point
in the tale he knows beforehand what is going to hap-

pen, because it is the sort of conclusion that he himself would choose. His is the delight of one artist recognizing another artist's master-hand.

The world of fantasy may be a topsy-turvy world, but it is one which children have always found particularly satisfying and logical. Nothing about it can unduly surprise them, since life is so full of surprises anyway and things very seldom turn out to be just what they seem. In an existence where so many things are strange and inexplicable—the transformation of a seed into a flower, the mystery of a lighted match, the fact that some objects float on water, while others for no apparent reason fall to the bottom—why should any one thing seem stranger than another? If a voice can and does come out of a wooden box, it should also come, far more appropriately, from a calico dog. Talking animals are an old convention by no means confined to childhood, and any toy once taken to the heart assumes a character and personality which needs only the lightest touch of fancy to bring it into life and action.

The imaginative story has a function deeper than that of entertainment alone. It shows life from a new angle, like objects seen through a prism. It can open fresh ranges of vision and understanding, rouse the perception of beauty in hitherto disregarded things. It has power through the simple magic of humor to rob childhood of a good many of its fears and bugaboos, for once you have laughed at anything in reassuring company it no longer has power to frighten you, and behind all nonsense there is somewhere a sound sanity. Moreover, it teaches, far more acceptably than the realistic story,

sympathy and unselfishness, the value of laughter, and
a certain happy tolerance with the foibles and foolish-
ness of other people. In the fairy tale it is usually the
over-clever and malicious who get their come-uppings,
the humble of heart who inherit the earth.

Imagination, more than any other quality, makes for
understanding and a regard for the feelings of others.
The child who has learned to look upon his own toys
as something more than mere sawdust and stuffing is
inclined to have respect for other people's treasures as
well as his own and to respect the sentiment that values
them; the child who meets frogs and kittens and puppies as individualized characters in his favorite storybook is not likely to be careless and unfeeling towards
animals in everyday life. Wonder and mystery are the
elements of life and growth all around us. Nothing in
any story can actually add to the magic of the world as
a child sees it, but it can help him towards new percep-
tions, fresh discoveries of his own.

*Told Under the Magic Umbrella* is a collection of
modern fanciful tales, widely representative and chosen
each for its particular appeal. *Ask Mr. Bear* has long
been a nursery classic, forerunner of many delightful
tales in which Marjorie Flack shows an unfailing sense
of the story needs of young children and of the dra-
matic elements that most appeal to them. *Two Little
Shoes* by Carol Ryrie Brink and Emma Brock's *Gingham Lena* both hinge on the homely magic by which
inanimate things take life and personality. Gingham
Lena, smudgy, carefree and adventurous, may well
stand for the spirit of rag dolls the world over, and, by

the way, it is not for nothing that the rag doll, and not her more elaborate sister, figures usually in the best-loved doll stories. Both Gelett Burgess, in *The Three Elevators,* and Caroline Emerson have the grand idea of bringing modern inventions and mechanical devices into line, so to speak, in the child's imaginative world by investing them with personal character. In Caroline Emerson's "Merry-Go-Round of Modern Tales" the car, the steam roller, the telephone, and other familiar objects suddenly decide to take matters into their own hands, with startling results. *The Merry-Go-Round and the Griggses* is one of the best of these irresistibly humorous tales.

Magic and wisdom are the time-honored attributes of the storybook cat. In *The Cobbler's Tale* it takes a cat to hit upon the simple device that makes the King's shoes comfortable. The ten-times granddaughter of this same cat is one of many endearing characters in "Rag-man of Paris," the refreshingly droll and genial story by Elizabeth Orton Jones from which this little tale is taken. Hope Newell's *Little Old Woman* is close kin to the wise men of Gotham and has a long ancestry among the more kindly forms of folklore humor. How to keep her geese warm is one of the problems which she solves by a system of patient and simple-minded reasoning. All children love paradoxes, and behind the laughter in this tale they will appreciate a kind of commonsense logic not so far different from their own.

Two of the stories in this volume have an African background, *Sojo* by Erick Berry and *The Bojabi Tree* by Edith Rickert, the latter being an adapted folk tale. African folklore is particularly rich in drama and action; animals play a more important part than humans in its legendry, and its nearness to primitive nature gives it a special interest to children. In "Rootabaga Stories" Carl Sandburg created a whole new folklore almost overnight—tales spontaneous, fresh as the prairie wind and colored through and through with the feeling of the American soil. Told in vigorous homespun prose, they bring to every child a sense of the magic of his own time and country. The Californian fairy tales of Monica Shannon, too, are definitely native in quality; one feels that they have grown directly out of their own environment.

One of the first tests of a good story is that it can be read or told aloud. It must hold its audience. The tales collected under the *Magic Umbrella* have all stood this test successfully, not once but many times.

MARGERY BIANCO

# CONTENTS

## ASK MR. BEAR

ONCE THERE WAS a boy named Danny. One day Danny's mother had a birthday.

Danny said to himself, "What shall I give my mother for her birthday?"

So Danny started out to see what he could find.

He walked along, and he met a Hen.

"Good morning, Mrs. Hen," said Danny. "Can you give me something for my mother's birthday?"

"Cluck, cluck," said the Hen. "I can give you a nice fresh egg for your mother's birthday."

"Thank you," said Danny, "but she has an egg."

"Let's see what we can find then," said the Hen.

So Danny and the Hen skipped along until they met a Goose.

"Good morning, Mrs. Goose," said Danny. "Can you give me something for my mother's birthday?"

1

"Honk, honk," said the Goose. "I can give you some nice feathers to make a fine pillow for your mother's birthday."

"Thank you," said Danny, "but she has a pillow."

"Let's see what we can find then," said the Goose.

So Danny and the Hen and the Goose all hopped along until they met a Goat.

"Good morning, Mrs. Goat," said Danny. "Can you give me something for my mother's birthday?"

"Maa, maa," said the Goat. "I can give you milk for making cheese."

"Thank you," said Danny, "but she has some cheese."

"Let's see what we can find then," said the Goat.

So Danny and the Hen and the Goose and the Goat all galloped along until they met a Sheep.

"Good morning, Mrs. Sheep," said Danny. "Can you give me something for my mother's birthday?"

"Baa, baa," said the Sheep. "I can give you some wool to make a warm blanket for your mother's birthday."

"Thank you," said Danny, "but she has a blanket."

"Let's see what we can find then," said the Sheep.

So Danny and the Hen and the Goose and the Goat and the Sheep all trotted along until they met a Cow.

"Good morning, Mrs. Cow," said Danny. "Can you give me something for my mother's birthday?"

"Moo, moo," said the Cow. "I can give you some milk and cream."

"Thank you," said Danny, "but she has some milk and cream."

"Then ask Mr. Bear," said the Cow. "He lives in the woods over the hill."

"All right," said Danny. "Let's go ask Mr. Bear."

"No," said the Hen.

"No," said the Goose.

"No," said the Goat.

"No," said the Sheep.

"No—no," said the Cow.

So Danny went alone to find Mr. Bear.

He ran and he ran until he came to a hill, and he walked and he walked until he came to the woods and there he met—Mr. Bear.

"Good morning, Mr. Bear," said Danny. "Can you give me something for my mother's birthday?"

"Hum, hum," said the Bear. "I have nothing to give you for your mother's birthday, but I can tell you something you can give her."

So Mr. Bear whispered a secret in Danny's ear.

"Oh," said Danny. "Thank you, Mr. Bear!"

Then he ran through the woods and he skipped down the hill and he came to his house.

"Guess what I have for your birthday!" Danny said to his mother.

So his mother tried to guess.

"Is it an egg?"

"No, it isn't an egg," said Danny.

"Is it a pillow?"

"No, it isn't a pillow," said Danny.

"Is it a cheese?"

"No, it isn't a cheese," said Danny.

"Is it a blanket?"

"No, it isn't a blanket," said Danny.

"Is it milk or cream?"

"No, it isn't milk or cream," said Danny.

His mother could not guess at all. So—Danny gave his mother

        a Big Birthday

            Bear Hug.

*By Marjorie Flack*

## LITTLE DUCKLING TRIES HIS VOICE

ONCE UPON A TIME fat Little Duckling went on a journey into the Wide World. He wandered along the Barnyard Road, and presently he saw the Kitty Cat.

"Me-ow!" said the Kitty Cat.

"O-o-oh!" cried Little Duckling. "Isn't that a *pretty* sound! I think I'll talk that way!"

But do you suppose Little Duckling could say "Me-ow"?

No indeed!

He tried, but the best he could do was: "Me-e-ack! Me-e-ack!"

And that wasn't pretty at all!

So Little Duckling waddled on and on. After a while he saw Puppy Dog.

"Bow-wow," said Puppy Dog.

"O-o-oh!" cried Little Duckling. "Isn't that a *lovely* noise! I think I'll talk that way!"

But do you suppose Little Duckling could say "Bow-wow"?

No indeed!

5

He tried, but this is the way he sounded: "B-ack! B-ack!" And that wasn't lovely at all!

Then Little Duckling waddled on and on. Soon he saw a Yellow Bird in a tree.

"Tweet-tweet-tweet-tweet tweet!" said Yellow Bird.

"Oh, oh, oh!" sighed Little Duckling. "Isn't that a *sweet* song! I think I'll sing that way!"

But do you suppose Little Duckling could sing "Tweet-Tweet"?

No indeed!

He tried his very best, but all he could say was: "Twack! Twack!"

And that wasn't sweet at all!

So Little Duckling waddled on and on. After a while he met Big Cow.

"Moo-o-o!" said Big Cow.

"O-o-oh!" thought Little Duckling. "Isn't that a *beautiful* roar! I think I'll roar that way!"

But do you suppose Little Duckling could say "Moo-o-o"?

He tried, but all he could manage to say was: "M-ack! M-ack!"

And that wasn't beautiful at all!

Little Duckling was very sad. He could not say "Me-ow" like Kitty Cat. He could not say "Bow-wow" like Puppy Dog. He could not say "Tweet-tweet" like Yellow Bird. He could not say "Moo-o-o" like Big Cow.

He waddled slowly on and on. All at once he saw his own Mother Duck coming toward him along the Barnyard Road.

"Quack! Quack!" cried Mother Duck.

"O-o-oh!" whispered happy Little Duckling to himself. "That is the prettiest sound in the whole Wide World! I think I'll talk *that* way!"

And he found he could say "Quack! Quack!" very nicely.

*By Marjorie La Fleur*

# TWO LITTLE SHOES

ALL WINTER Sally Lou's two little shoes had carried
her up and down stairs, back and forth to school, and
out to play. They felt very important and proud. For
how could Sally go to school or run errands for Mother
or play hop-scotch without their help? The more
wrinkled and scuffed they grew, the prouder they became.

"We have grown old in Sally Lou's service," said
one to the other. "She could certainly never get along
without us!"

"She changes her stockings every day, and she has
even put away her winter coat," said the other, "but
she could never, never get along without us."

Then one day Mother said: "Sally Lou, I'm going
to take you downtown today." The two little shoes
jumped for joy when they heard Mother speak, and
they cried: "Oh, goody!" and "Hurray!" just as Sally

Lou did. They carried Sally Lou away to get ready, and soon they were trotting side by side to town. Into a great big store they went, and the little shoes were just as much interested in looking at everything as Sally Lou herself. They kept stopping to admire things, and Mother had to hurry them along.

At last they came to the strangest place of all, for it was entirely full of little shoes. Shoe-button eyes gazed at them from all sides, wide-mouthed pumps seemed to smile at them, and one impudent play-shoe stuck out its tongue. Suddenly Sally Lou's shoes began to feel how worn and shabby they looked among all these shining patent leathers and fine new shoes.

"Sally Lou really should have polished us before bringing us into such high society," they said. Then the terrible truth dawned upon them. Sally Lou's Mother was buying her a brand new pair of shoes! The shoe man took them off and cast them aside while Sally Lou tried on pair after pair of darling pumps and sandals and slippers.

"Those flimsy things will never keep her warm," groaned the two little shoes. But nobody paid the slightest attention to them. At last Sally Lou and Mother found a shiny pair of strap slippers that were just what they wanted.

"Oh, may I please wear them?" begged Sally Lou.

"I believe you may," said Mother, "if the gentleman will be so kind as to wrap up the old ones." So Sally Lou's two little shoes were wrapped in a brown paper parcel and carried home. They grumbled a good deal about the string and paper being too tight. But that was not the real trouble with them. Their poor hearts were nearly broken because Sally Lou had put them aside for a pair of slippers. When they got home they were unwrapped and set side by side in Sally Lou's closet.

"Well," said Sally Lou's winter coat, hanging above them, "I see you're here at last. I thought you were never coming."

"How can she skip and play without us?" cried the little shoes. "And won't she catch cold in those silly little slippers?"

"It's spring now," said the winter coat. "We've had our day." The little shoes sighed and flopped dejectedly on the closet floor. But they couldn't help dreaming of the good times they were missing.

And when the summer dresses began talking about the picnic, they couldn't help listening.

"I'm sure she's going to wear me," said the little sleeveless dress, "and it will be such fun!"

"Oh, I do wish she'd choose me," sighed the blue gingham. "There's nothing I like better than a picnic." The two little shoes cuddled closer together.

"We used to go to everything," they whispered. "Oh, how we should like to go to the picnic! But that is all over now."

The night before the picnic the dresses were squabbling and arguing all night as to which was going next day. The new strap slippers, which had been set in the closet for the night, laughed scornfully.

"There is only one thing certain about it," they said, "she is *sure* to wear *us!*"

They were all making so much noise that they didn't hear the patter of the raindrops on the roof. It rained all night. When Sally Lou got up the next morning she began to cry. The dresses all hung limp and dejected. It looked as if there wouldn't be any picnic that day.

But presently they heard Sally Lou laughing and singing again.

"It's clearing! It's clearing!" she sang as she danced up the stairs. "And Mother says I may go, if I'll wear my little old shoes to keep my feet warm and dry. Where are you, little old shoes? We're going on the picnic!" The little old shoes sat up as stiffly as they could, and as soon as Sally Lou put them on they began to dance. Oh! how they danced! They had never been gayer or happier in their lives, or carried Sally Lou through livelier adventures. The weather continued to clear and the picnic was a great success.

And after that the two little shoes never minded being put away in the closet. For they thought:

"Someday Sally Lou will be sure to need us again. If it hadn't been for us, she couldn't have gone on the picnic."

*By Carol Ryrie Brink*

## GINGHAM LENA

ONCE UPON A TIME there was a little boy named Elmer who had a little sister Selma. They lived with their father and mother in a white farmhouse with a porch in the front and a pump under a windmill at the back. On the farm there were twenty cows and twenty pigs and some chickens and two dozen big fields that rolled away over the hills and were covered with wheat and corn and potatoes. There was a silo and a plow and other farm things.

Selma had a doll with blue eyes, orange wool hair and a smudgy nose. Her name was Brin Hilda and her nose was smudgy because she ate mud pies. Elmer had a gingham dog called Lena. She ate ants sometimes if they waited long enough.

One day Selma could not find Brin Hilda anywhere. She and Elmer looked in the house under the radio and in the barn under the hay and in the seats of the old black car. They could not find Brin Hilda anywhere.

Selma sat down on one side of the pump and twisted her face up to keep from crying. Elmer put his hands in his pockets and sat down on the other side of the pump and kicked dirt with his bare toes. They could not think where Brin Hilda could be. Gingham Lena sat by the pump, too, and thought and thought.

Oh, Brin Hilda, with your smudgy face, where have you gone and what are you doing?

Then Lena smiled and said to herself, "I'll just go out and find Brin Hilda. She must be somewhere."

So Gingham Lena cocked up one ear and ran over to the chicken yard to ask the chickens.

"Have you seen Brin Hilda?" she cried out.

But the chickens were too busy pecking and clucking to notice anything.

"No, Gingham Lena, we have not seen her," they said.

Lena cocked up her other ear and ran into the barn to ask the horses and cows. But the horses were out in the field working and the cows were far away eating in the pasture.

Then she cocked both ears at once and ran out of the barn again and right into a big gray goose who was peering in at the barn door with her neck stretched way out.

"Have you seen Brin Hilda?" asked Lena.

"No, Gingham Lena," said the goose, "I have not seen her."

And the turkeys in the field had not seen Brin Hilda. And the red squirrel in the tree had not seen her either. Nor had the pigs who were grubbing in the pig yard.

"No, we have not seen her, Gingham Lena," each one of them answered.

Gingham Lena sat down by the pig yard fence and thought and thought.

Oh, Brin Hilda, with your smudgy face, where have you gone and what are you doing?

Then Lena wagged her tail and ran over to the duck pond, where the ducks were cleaning their feathers.

"Have you—" cried Lena, and she slipped in the mud and splashed into the pond. She went bump down to the bottom, but as she was stuffed with cotton, she bobbed up again in a second. The ducks fished her out and set her in the sun to dry.

"Have you seen Brin Hilda?" gasped Lena between the drops that trickled down her nose.

"No, Gingham Lena," said the ducks, "we have not seen her."

Gingham Lena sat in the sun drying and thought and thought about a place where Brin Hilda could be.

Oh, Brin Hilda, Brin Hilda, with your smudgy face, where have you gone and what are you doing?

"Have you asked the scarecrow?" said the ducks. "He sees everything that happens around here."

"Oh, thanks," said Lena, and she raced around the pond through the apple orchard. She ran between the bee hives by the sweet clover field and bumped into one of the hives in her hurry. And all the bees flew buzzing out and chased her. Lena ran as fast as she could with bees sitting on her nose and bees sitting on her tail and everywhere. But when they found she was only cotton, they flew back home.

At last she came to the corn field.

"Have you seen Brin Hilda?" she cried.

But the scarecrow had not seen Brin Hilda anywhere, not for days and days. The last he had seen of her was the bow on her apron one day last week.

Lena ran up and down and back and forth between the corn rows looking, but she could not see a bit of Brin Hilda either. She lay down all tired out and tried to think of a place where Brin Hilda might be hiding.

"I must find her somewhere," said Lena, "or Selma will be crying for lonesomeness."

She thought and thought.

Oh, Brin Hilda, Brin Hilda, with your smudgy face, where have you gone and what are you doing?

Then suddenly she smiled and cocked her ears and wagged her tail and ran off toward the wild-blackberry patch. She jumped over the ditch and dashed along the highway past Nokomis Lake and Yellow Butter Farm, and the white church and the schoolhouse of Blooming Valley. She ran past a gopher sitting by the roadside and under a meadow lark singing on the telegraph wire, and past the field of hazel nut bushes and into the blackberry patch all out of breath. She sniffed around the bushes and scratched her gingham sides on the stickers.

Then she caught sight of someone in a pink bonnet, someone sitting with her back that way.

"Have you seen Brin Hilda," shouted Lena.

She thought she heard someone giggle, but the person in the pink bonnet did not say a word.

Lena started toward her, but one blackberry bramble was holding her on one side and more blackberry brambles were holding her on the other side. Lena jerked this way and that and tore a hole in her gingham.

"Selma has a thimble and she can mend that," said Lena.

And she ran around to peep into the pink bonnet. And there inside of it were Brin Hilda's blue eyes and smudgy nose, as plain as plain could be!

"So that is where you are," said Lena. "You come along home!"

And Gingham Lena ran back through the brambles out of the blackberry patch with Brin Hilda balanced on her back.

She ran along the highway past the schoolhouse and the church of Blooming Valley and past Yellow Butter Farm and Nokomis Lake and over the ditch into the corn field. She bounced past the scarecrow who waved his sleeves at her, through the orchard and around the duck pond between the geese and the turkeys. The pigs squealed and the ducks quacked and the turkeys gobbled and all the birds sang.

Lena dashed toward the pump where Selma and Elmer were sitting. Selma had her hands in her eyes and the tears were running into her mouth. Elmer was throwing stones at the back fence.

Lena pranced up crying, "Here we are, here we are!"

And when they saw who was coming, the children

shouted loudly. Selma hugged Brin Hilda up in her arms and Elmer patted Lena on her cotton head and said, "Good dog, good dog!"

Gingham Lena wiggled herself all over—and they lived happily ever after.

*By Emma L. Brock*

## THE MERRY-GO-ROUND AND THE
## GRIGGSES

THE MERRY-GO-ROUND whirled round and round and
the music played. The horses and the ponies and the
zebras rose and fell on their shiny poles as they dashed
past. The Griggses watched the merry-go-round and
the merry-go-round watched the Griggses. Every last
Griggs was there and never had the merry-go-round
seen them look so happy and triumphant, and he had
seen them every day since he had come to town.

*But today was different from any other day.* There
was joy and excitement in the heart of every Griggs; in
the heart of Mary Griggs, aged eleven; in the heart of
Tommy Griggs, aged nine; likewise in Betty Griggs,

aged seven, and in Billy Griggs, aged five. The same feelings were equally alive in Jennie and Jimmie, the twins, aged four. For today each Griggs held five cents gripped in his right hand. *They were going to ride on the merry-go-round!*

"I'm glad that they got the money together in time," thought the merry-go-round. "It's my last day here. I suppose those bigger two had to earn it for the whole crew. Five, ten, fifteen, twenty, twenty-five, thirty," he counted as he whirled by. "They had to get thirty cents just for one ride. That *is* a lot!"

The merry-go-round felt himself go slowly and more slowly. It was time for him to stop. The people who were riding the horses and the ponies climbed down and the boy jumped off the zebra.

"He seemed to think he could make me go faster by kicking me," complained the zebra. "I'm glad his money is all used up."

"You shouldn't mind things so much," said the merry-go-round comfortingly. "He hasn't hurt your paint any."

Then came the Griggses. They swarmed over the merry-go-round like a drove of monkeys. They tried every horse and they tried every seat before they were satisfied. Mary and Tommy lifted the twins into one of the coaches and told them to sit very still, which they did not do. They hung over the edge and shouted. Tommy mounted a gallant black charger and Mary chose a milk white steed. Betty climbed on to the complaining zebra and Billy upon a brown pony. But Billy very soon fell off and they put him into the coach with the twins.

"All aboard!" whistled the merry-go-round. "Hang on tight. I'm starting!"

The merry-go-round man shut the gates so that no one else could enter. The music began to play. The engine started and away they went.

At first the Griggses sat very still. They hung on as tight as they could and did not say a word. Things felt a little strange and queer to the Griggses. The merry-go-round was disappointed.

"Aren't they going to like me?" A fear crept into the valves of the merry-go-round. "Have they waited a whole week and earned thirty cents and then aren't they going to like me? Oh, dearie me!" sighed the merry-go-round.

But a few turns more and his doubts vanished. The Griggses were becoming accustomed to the new motion and they began to shout to each other. You could hear them even above the music. Round and round they spun. Up and down went the horses. The Griggses became more and more exhilarated.

"I can change horses," shouted Tommy. "Watch me!"

He swung over to the next mount. The others cheered.

"I can ride without holding on," screamed Betty.

"Not for long," said the zebra as she promptly fell off and had to be picked up and put back on again by the merry-go-round man.

The merry-go-round was quite satisfied. Carrying Griggses was a pleasure to him.

But the best of things must end. The merry-go-round
had gone as far as he ever went for a five cent fare. The
music stopped. The merry-go-round ran slowly and
more slowly. The ride was over. The Griggses had no
more five cents. They would have to get off!

They climbed down quietly, every last Griggs of
them. Even the twins at four knew that "no more"
meant *no more* with the Griggses. They did not even
cry.

Then a strange thing happened.

"I have been doing just what that merry-go-round
man has told me to do ever since I was a child," said
the merry-go-round. "To-day for once I'm going to do
what I want to do. I don't care if I have given them a
five cent ride. I'm not going to stop! *I'm going to keep
right on going!*"

So instead of stopping the merry-go-round went
faster and faster until he was whirling around as before, with the music playing and the flags flying.

"Stop!" shouted the merry-go-round man as he ran
round and round after the merry-go-round; but no
good did shouting do him.

"*Stop!*" shouted all the people who were waiting to
get on, and they ran round and round the merry-go-
round; but no good did shouting do them.

"*Keep on going!*" shouted all the Griggses and that
is just what the merry-go-round did do.

The children climbed back to their places. The
horses rose higher than they had ever risen before. The
music played louder than ever. Never in the days of
merry-go-rounds was there such a ride!

When the merry-go-round could run no longer for want of steam and the music could play no longer for want of breath, they both had to stop. Off tumbled the Griggses. They had had five times as much ride as they had expected. The merry-go-round man was very cross but there was nothing to do about that.

The Griggses jumped to the ground, but—they were so dizzy that they could scarcely stand. Indeed, they did not stand long. The twins laughed and sat down heavily. Mary fell over them, while Betty and Billy hung on to the turnstile. The trees and the houses spun round and round. All that the children could do was to sit on the ground and laugh.

The merry-go-round man was worried. Whatever was he going to do with them? He picked them up carefully and put them on their feet and started them off toward home.

"Good-by," they shouted back to the merry-go-round, "and thank you!"

"Don't mention it," chuckled the merry-go-round as he started off with his new load of passengers.

He watched them out of sight. The twins sat down twice and had to be picked up and put on their feet again. And this is the way their tracks looked all the way down the street.

*By Caroline D. Emerson*

## GOOSEBERRY GARDEN

ONCE THERE WAS a beautiful green garden. In the garden there lived a lady, and her name was Mrs. Gooseberry.

And the green grass grew all around.

Now in the beautiful green garden there was a lovely house. In the house there were ever so many windows. In the windows were children peeping out. Their name was Gooseberry, too.

And the green grass grew all around.

Now in the lovely house there was a room with a big, big window. In the window there hung a golden cage. In the cage there was a little green bird. All day long it sang a merry tune.

And the green grass grew all around.

In the garden the Gooseberry children played. Sometimes Mrs. Gooseberry opened the door of the cage and the little green bird flew out. It sat on their shoulders and ate from their hands. It flew above their heads and sang its merry tune. Always at night it flew back into its cage and went to sleep.

And the green grass grew all around.

One morning Mrs. Gooseberry woke up very early. The sun was rising over the hills. All was still. She looked, and what did she see? The little green bird was gone from its cage. The door was unhooked and standing open. The breeze blew in the open window.

And the green grass grew all around.

Mrs. Gooseberry called the children and they all jumped out of bed. The biggest Gooseberry children hunted, the middle-sized Gooseberry children called, the littlest Gooseberry children cried, but the little green bird was gone.

And the green grass grew all around.

At last the Gooseberry children sat down to eat their breakfast. A very sad meal it was. The porridge had lumps, the milk would spill, and the sugar bowl was empty. Worst of all, there was no little green bird to sing its merry tune.

And the green grass grew all around.

The Gooseberry children ran outdoors. "We will find the little green bird," said the biggest Gooseberry child to the littlest. "We will, we will," said all the Gooseberry children together. So they hitched up the pony to the cart and started off at a trot. They drove round and round the garden wall, looking and listening.

And the green grass grew all around.

Now in Gooseberry Garden there was a pond. In the pond there was an island. On the island there was a tree. Mrs. Gooseberry wheeled the baby up and down and back and forth over the little bridge, for his nap, while the children hunted.

And the green grass grew all around.

Soon the children grew tired and the pony grew tired, for they could not find the little green bird. Back through the garden gate they came to ask their mother what they should do next. Mrs. Gooseberry smiled and said: "Perhaps the little green bird is very near. Perhaps it is right here in the garden!"

And the green grass grew all around.

So the Gooseberry children kept on hunting. The first day they looked in the orchard. They climbed up ladders. They shook down apples. They slid down trunks of trees. But no little bird was there.

And the green grass grew all around.

But the children kept on hunting. The second day they looked in the vegetable patch. They lifted up the rhubarb leaves. They shook the tomato branches. They pulled up the cabbages. But no little bird was there.

And the green grass grew all around.

Still the Gooseberry children kept on hunting. The third day they looked in the flower beds. They peered in the rosebushes. They filled their aprons with daisies. They tipped over flower pots. But no little bird was there.

And the green grass grew all around.

At last the Gooseberry children had to give up. The little green bird was really gone. Suddenly they heard a merry tune coming from the island. Over the bridge they ran as fast as they could go. Up, up they looked. In the tree there was a branch. On the branch there was a nest. On the nest there was a little green bird.

And the green grass grew all around.

When they saw the little green bird on the nest, with four baby birds peeping their heads out, they were very happy. They held hands and danced round the tree. And this is the song they sang:

"The bird was on the nest,
The nest was on the branch,
The branch was on the limb,
The limb was on the tree,
The tree was on the island,
The island was in the pond,
The pond was in the garden,
And the green grass grew all around, around, around,
And the green grass grew all around."

*By Lois Lenski*

## THE COBBLER'S TALE

A LONG TIME AGO there lived a king who had very big feet. Everybody knew it. And everybody knew that the king never laughed. But who would laugh if he were a king with feet so big that he could have only one pair of shoes?

One day a cobbler was called to the palace. The king took his one pair of shoes from a place called ROYAL SHOE CLOSET.

He said to the cobbler, "The right shoe you must stitch all around, and the left one you must make comfy, for my royal great toe is very tender. Now, mind they be done by tomorrow! A king must not go barefooted for more than a day."

"Very well," said the cobbler. And he took away the shoes.

He stitched and he stitched all around the right shoe. But when he came to the left shoe he began to scratch his head.

"How can I make it comfy?" he thought. And the more he thought the more he scratched his head.

Then his little boy said, "What would happen, sir, if you *didn't* make the king's shoe comfy before tomorrow?"

"Tsck! Both our heads would be chopped off!" said the cobbler, scratching his head again.

The little boy was very much afraid. He ran to the palace. He ran to the guardroom. He ran to the house of the king's best wigmaker. But nobody knew what to do.

The last thing before he went to bed that night, the little boy whispered into the ear of a wise old cat with green whiskers, "Please, my dear, try to think of some way to make the king's shoe comfy!"

Now all wise cats, and perhaps other cats, too, take fur from their own soft coats to make their babies' beds comfy.

The next morning the cobbler stopped scratching his head. "Look!" he cried.

And the little boy jumped out of bed to see.

The king's left shoe was not only lined with fur, but

it held six new kittens, sound asleep. And the wise old cat with green whiskers was very proud indeed.

"Just the thing!" said the cobbler, as he took the kittens out of the shoe and set them down by their wise old mother.

*"Just the thing!"* said the little boy, for he loved kittens.

"JUST THE THING!" said the king as he sat upon his throne, wearing his fur-lined shoe. And all of a sudden his majesty began to laugh!

Then the first row of courtiers began to smile. The second row began to snicker. The third row began to titter. And the fourth row rolled on the floor.

And the Lord High Chancellor in charge of titles and holidays said, "Let there be a holiday throughout the land because the king is laughing!"

"Three cheers!" shouted the courtiers.

"Let the cobbler who made the king's shoe comfy," continued the Lord High Chancellor, "be made cobbler to all France."

The courtiers shouted again.

So the cobbler became a famous man. But after that the wise old cat with green whiskers, and her six new kittens, too, lived with the cobbler and the little boy, and ate the best they had. For it was she who had saved their lives by making the king's shoe comfy.

*By Elizabeth Orton Jones*

# THE LAMB THAT WENT TO FAIRYLAND

THERE WAS ONCE a fairy who took a great fancy to a tiny white lamb. He really was a dear little creature, and I don't wonder she fell in love with him. She used often to come and visit with him in the meadow where he lived with his mother, and she was very anxious to take him to a fairy party some evening.

The little lamb was shy. "What do you do at the parties?" he asked.

"Oh, dance mostly," said the fairy.

But the little lamb explained that he didn't know how to dance.

"I will soon teach you," said the fairy.

So she came every evening when her day's work was done and showed the little lamb how to dance, and he soon learned to skip about quite nicely.

At last a day came when the fairy took him off to the party, but his mother made him promise to come back the next morning. She knew the ways of fairies.

He enjoyed himself tremendously.

All the fairies admired him very much. They thought his coat so beautifully white and soft; they loved his little black nose and quaint woodeny legs. He gave them all rides on his back in turn (even the Fairy Queen had one), and when the time for dancing came he did very well indeed and astonished them all with his pretty steps. When he left, the Fairy Queen presented him with a garland of daisies. "They are fairy flowers," she said. "They will never fade, and so long as you wear them you will remain young."

When the lamb got home he had great tales to tell about his happy adventures, so that he became quite a celebrity and everyone made such a fuss over him that he got rather proud and silly, and after a very short time would hardly speak to his friends.

Of course this vexed them very much, and the wicked old rat who lived in the mill-pond and was always ready to do anyone an ill turn, suggested a way to pay him out for his pride. "While he is asleep I will gnaw through his gay garland that he is so proud of," she said, "and when he goes out walking he will lose it." All of which happened just as she planned. And so the foolish lamb lost his fairy garland and grew older like any other lamb.

His friend the fairy did not come to see him for some time. She was very busy helping on the spring things, and had no time for visiting. When she did come again she was very disappointed to find that the lamb had grown into quite a good-sized sheep, fat and comfortable. His wool was no longer downy and white, and he had entirely forgotten how to dance.

"Where is your magic garland?" said the fairy. And he had to confess he had lost it.

The fairy went back to her friends. She really did not feel that a big solemn sheep would be very welcome at their revels. But every year in the early spring when the new lambs are born, their mothers tell the story of the lamb that was invited to Fairyland, and they all go skipping about in the meadows practicing their dancing steps.

Each of them hopes that he may one day find the magic garland, and never grow old and staid, and be able to go a-visiting to Fairyland. After all, it must be lying about somewhere; so if you find it, you will know what to do with it, won't you? But be sure to give it **to** a lamb with a black nose. They're so much the prettiest.

*By Rose Fyleman*

## LITTLE DOG AND BIG DOG

ONCE UPON A TIME there were two dogs who were great friends. One of them was small and one of them was large, and they were called Little Dog and Big Dog all the days of their lives, and had no other names.

Little Dog barked at everything he saw. He barked at the cat and he barked at the kittens; he barked at the cow and he barked at the calf; he barked at his own shadow; and he even barked at the moon in the sky with a "Bow-wow-wow!" and a "Bow-wow-wow!"

Big Dog had a very loud bark, "Bow-wow!" "Bow-wow!" but he barked only when he had something to say. And everybody listened to him.

Now one day as the two dogs sat together in the sunshine, Big Dog said to Little Dog:

"Come, let us go to see our friend, the king."

Little Dog thought this was a splendid plan, and they started at once.

Big Dog walked along the road with his tail curled over his back, and his head held high. "There is no need of haste," he said, but Little Dog thought there must be.

"I shall get there first," he called, as he scampered ahead, but presently he came back as fast as he had gone.

"Oh, Big Dog, Big Dog," he said, "we cannot go to see the king."

"Why not?" asked Big Dog. "Has he gone away from home?"

"I know nothing about that," answered Little Dog, who was almost out of breath, "but a little farther on there is a great river, and we can never get across."

But Big Dog would not turn back. "I must see this great river," he said, and he walked on as quietly as before. Little Dog followed him, and when they came to the river Big Dog jumped in, splish! splash! and began to swim.

"Wait, wait," cried Little Dog, but Big Dog only answered, "Don't be afraid."

So in jumped Little Dog, splish! splash! too, for he did not want to be left behind. He was terribly frightened, but he paddled himself along with his four feet just as he saw Big Dog doing, and when he was safe across the river, which was not half so wide as he had thought, he barked at it as if he had never been afraid at all.

"Bow-wow-wow-wow! You cannot keep us from the king," he said, and he was off and away before Big Dog had shaken the water from his coat. But in less time than it takes to tell it, Big Dog spied him running back, with his tail hanging down and his ears drooping.

"Oh, Big Dog, Big Dog!" he cried. "We cannot go

to see the king, for in the wood yonder there is a bear, and she will eat us both for her supper. I heard her say so myself."

Then Big Dog made haste to the wood, barking loudly:

"Bow-wow! Bow-wow! I am not afraid! I am not afraid!" and when the bear heard him she ran to her home as fast as she could.

"I can eat honey for my supper," she said; and the two dogs saw no more of her.

Now by this time Little Dog had run so fast and barked so much that he was tired. "I do not want to go to see the king," he said; and he lay down in the road and put his head between his two front paws.

But Big Dog said, "I smell a bone," and Little Dog jumped up in a hurry again. Sniff! Sniff!—where could it be? The two dogs put their noses close to the ground and followed the scent till they came to the turn of the road; and there sat a charcoal burner eating his supper of bread and mutton chops by his fire.

Little Dog wanted to run up and beg for something, but Big Dog would not go with him. "It is more polite to wait," he said; and he sat down on the other side of the road. Little Dog sat down beside him, and they waited and waited; but at last the man finished his chops and threw the bones to the dogs, which was just what Big Dog had hoped he would do. Oh, how good they tasted!

"Where shall we sleep tonight?" asked Little Dog when he had eaten his share.

"Oh, never fear," answered Big Dog, "we will find

a place"; and when they had gone on their way they very soon came to a house in the wood. The door was open, and Big Dog put his head inside to see if anybody was at home. Nobody lived there, however, but a barn swallow, so the dogs went in and lay down to rest on some hay in the corner.

"We must be off early," said Big Dog; but when they woke up the next morning the door was fastened tight; for the wind had blown by in the night and slammed it into its place. When Big Dog saw this he was in great distress.

"Oh, Little Dog! Little Dog!" he cried. "I fear we can never go to see the king, for the door is closed, and there is no one to open it."

"But we can go through the hole under the door," answered Little Dog; and when Big Dog looked, there, sure enough, at the bottom of the door, where a board had rotted away, was a hole just large enough for a little dog to creep through. Little Dog put his nose through and his head through, and then wriggle, wriggle, he was out and barking merrily.

"Come on, Big Dog," he called; but Big Dog could not go. He could not even get his head through the hole.

"You must go on alone," he said to Little Dog, "and when you have come to the king's palace, and have told him about me, perhaps he will send me aid."

But Little Dog did not wait until he reached the king's palace to ask for help. "Bow-wow-wow-wow! Listen to me," he barked, as he ran down the road. "Big Dog, my friend, is shut up in the house in the wood, and cannot go to see the king. Bow-wow-wow-wow!"

At first there were only birds to hear him, but presently he saw a woodcutter with an ax on his shoulder.

"Bow-wow-wow-wow! Listen to me," barked Little Dog. "Big Dog, my friend, is shut up in the house in the wood and cannot go to see the king. Bow-wow-wow-wow!" But the woodcutter did not understand a word he said.

"Whew! whew!" he whistled, which meant, "Come, little doggie, follow me"; but Little Dog had no time to play.

He hurried on as fast as he could, and by and by he met the woodcutter's wife going to town with a basket of eggs on her arm. "Bow-wow-wow-wow! Listen to me. Big Dog, my friend, is shut up in the house in the wood, and cannot go to see the king," barked Little Dog. But the woodcutter's wife did not understand a word he said.

"You noisy little dog," she cried. "You have startled me so that it is a wonder every egg in my basket is not broken," and she shook her skirts to get rid of him.

"Nobody will listen to me," thought Little Dog, as he scampered on, but just then he spied a little boy with a bundle of sticks on his back. He was the woodcutter's little boy; and—do you believe it?—he understood every word that Little Dog said, and followed him to the house.

When they drew near they heard Big Dog calling for help:

"Bow-wow! Bow-wow! Come and let me out. Come and let me out."

"Bow-wow! We are coming," answered Little Dog.

"We are coming," said the woodcutter's little boy; and the very next minute Big Dog was free.

The king's palace was not far from the wood, and the two dogs were soon at their journey's end. The king was so pleased to see them that he made a great feast for them, and invited the woodcutter's little boy because he was their friend.

After the feast Big Dog and Little Dog were sent home in the king's own carriage; and all the rest of their lives they were even better friends than before they went traveling together.

*By Maude Lindsay*

## SOJO

SOJO WAS ALWAYS sleepy. He woke up sleepy in the morning. He yawned all day long. He dropped asleep over his lunch; he slept halfway through his dinner. And if you'll believe it, he went to sleep when he should have been working.

One morning his Mammy called him early to get up and go down to the pool and bring back water for the cabbages. That, if you haven't guessed it, was on a Monday morning. Sojo rubbed his eyes and ate his breakfast and took his bowl and went down to the pool.

Pretty soon he lay down and began to finish his sleep. When he woke up, he heard something sper-lashing and sper-loshing in the water. Sojo yawned and rubbed his eyes; and there, right in the very middle of the pool, was a quite small Elephant, a-squirting water over his back from a quite small trunk.

"It must be fun to do that," said Sojo, yawning politely behind his hand.

"Not very," said the quite small Elephant. "It's too easy," and he squirted a trunkful of water into the bushes.

"Look here," said Sojo suddenly. "I know a place that would be just loads of fun to squirt water on. It's quite near here, too."

"Is that so?" asked the quite small Elephant eagerly. "Where is this place?"

But Sojo shook his head sleepily. "You wouldn't be interested," he decided after a moment; and he flopped back on the grass again and closed his eyes. The quite small Elephant was silent a moment. Then he squirted another trunkful of water into the bushes. Sojo opened one eye, ever so little.

The quite small Elephant came nearer.

"Hi!" he said. "What would you take to show me this place? I've been doing this every day for a whole week."

Sojo opened both eyes and sat up. "Oh, I wouldn't take anything for it. You're a friend of mine, and I'd be glad to show it to you. Mind you, it's a good game, but a sort of difficult one. I don't even know if you could do it. The game," he explained, getting to his feet, "is to take a trunkful of water from here— Follow me."

With the quite small Elephant carrying a trunkful of water, Sojo went along the path to the garden where the cabbages grew.

"You see, this is the game," explained Sojo. "You spray the water ve-ry carefully over the cabbages. If you spray it too hard and root up a cabbage, you lose a point. And if you don't bring enough water and the cabbages dry up, you lose the game. But if you bring four trunkfuls a morning every morning and make this place a nice swimmy marsh, it's a beautiful game."

"That does sound fun," said the quite small Elephant gratefully. "Like this?" and he sent out the water from his trunk in a long wish-h, whoo-o-sh all over the cabbages.

Sojo watched with his head on one side. "Not bad for a first try. But it's only fair."

"I think I could do better next time," said the quite small Elephant anxiously. And he could. And he did. Sojo leaned against a tree; and when the Elephant had used up the fourth trunkful of water, he woke up again.

"That was very good indeed," he said. "And no doubt you'll do better tomorrow."

"Please, can't I do just one more?" asked the Elephant.

But Sojo shook his head. "Oh, no. Four tries every morning is all you can have. That's the rule of the game. Now come back tomorrow and see how much better you can do."

"Well, thank you tremendously!" cried the quite small Elephant, and went away.

And Sojo slid down to the foot of the tree to finish his sleep. When his Mammy came to wake him, she certainly was surprised to see how nicely her cabbages had been watered.

Next morning Sojo's Mammy called him to get up and husk the corn. She said, "Take the corn down to the wide flat stone by the pool and pound the husks away." And that, if you haven't guessed it, was on a Tuesday morning.

Sojo rubbed his eyes and ate his breakfast. He took the corn in a basket down to the wide flat stone and sat down to look at it. Pretty soon he rolled over and began to finish his sleep.

When he woke up, he saw straight ahead of him in the pool two e-normous nostrils, and two little pricky pink ears, and two small twinkly black eyes.

"Hi there, Hippo!" said Sojo, and he got to his feet and began to pound the corn with a long flail.

Pretty soon he felt a cool breath on his shoulder; and the Hippo sighed, "What are you doing there? Can't I do that, too?"

Sojo shook his head and kept right on pounding the corn with his flail. "This is just a game; you wouldn't be interested," he said.

"How do you know I wouldn't be interested?" asked the Hippo crossly. "I can do that as well as you can. Just let me try," and he started to shove Sojo off the rock. But Sojo was firm.

"No, it's a very difficult game; and you have to play it just so. Now run along and don't bother me."

The Hippo watched a little longer. Then he said,

"What would you take to let me play at that game, too? I bet I'd be good at it."

Sojo sighed and stopped pounding the corn. "If you want to play it, you walk round and round the rock, stamping on the corn. And when it's all stamped out, you blow on it, very gently, and blow all the husks into the water. And if you leave any husks, you lose a point; and if you blow away any corn, you lose the game. It's difficult, and I don't even know if you could do it."

"Oh, I could do it all right," said the Hippo in his big breathful voice. And he could. And he would. And he did. His four big flat feet were four times as big as Sojo's two feet and the flail. And he pounded out all the dry corn. And his breath was four times as strong as any little breeze and he blew away all the chaff into the water.

Sojo had lain down under a tree; and when he woke up, the Hippo said, "Now that's done. What do I do next?"

"You help me put it all in a basket, so. And I'll take it home. And the next time I play this game I'll let you know so that you can come and play it, too," said Sojo; and he went home, yawning, to his Mammy.

And she certainly was surprised to see how well her corn had been pounded.

Next morning Sojo's Mammy called him to get up and dig her a new garden. She said, "Get up. I want a garden dug down beyond the cabbages." And that, if you haven't guessed it, was on a Wednesday morning.

Sojo rubbed his eyes and ate his breakfast. He took his hoe and went down beyond the cabbages to dig the new garden. He sat down under a tree and looked at what he had to do, and pretty soon he rolled over and began to finish his sleep.

When he woke up, he heard the funniest grunting and sk-uff-ulufuling in the underbrush. So he yawned and sat up, and straight ahead of him was a dark snout and two bright black eyes poking out through the brush. And then a little bristly black Pig with two shiny white tusks followed the snout.

"Hi there, little black Pig!" said Sojo; and he got to his feet and began to dig busily with his hoe.

Pretty soon the little bristly black Pig asked, "What are you doing there? Can't I do that, too?"

Sojo shook his head and kept right on digging with his hoe. "This is just a game; you wouldn't be interested," he said.

"How do you know I wouldn't be interested?" asked the little bristly black Pig snappily. "I could do it as well as you could. Just you let me try."

But Sojo was firm. "No. It's a very difficult game, and you have to play it just so. Now run along and don't bother me."

The little Pig watched for a while longer; and then he said, "What would you take to let me play at that game, too? I bet I'd be good at it."

Sojo sighed and stopped digging with his hoe. "Oh, I wouldn't take anything for it. You're a friend of mine, but I don't know if you could do it," and he laid down his hoe and sat down under a tree.

But the little black Pig could. And he would. And he did. He began to dig with his tusks. He shoved and he pushed and he grunted and he scrabbled, and he went down one row of the garden. His two tusks were twice as sharp as Sojo's hoe and much, much faster. And he went down another row of the garden. And pretty soon he had finished it all.

Sojo had lain down under a tree; and when he woke up, the little bristly black Pig asked, "Now that's done. What am I to do next?"

"That's all there is," said Sojo. "But you played it very well. Come and play again sometime," and he went home, yawning, to his Mammy.

And she certainly was surprised to see how well her new garden had been hoed.

Next morning Sojo's Mammy called him to get up and cut the grass on the path to the road. She said, "The grass on the path to the road is too long to walk through." And that, if you haven't guessed it, was on a Thursday morning.

Sojo rubbed his eyes and ate his breakfast. He took his sickle and went off along the path to the roadway. He cut a few feet of grass, and then he sat down under a tree to look at what he had to do and began to finish his sleep.

When he woke up, he saw a white animal with black spots and two long black horns, eating the grass on the pathway.

"Hi there, Goat!" said Sojo; and he got to his feet and began to cut the grass with his sickle. After he had cut a little more, he began to gather it up, piece by piece, blade by blade, and bind it together into a small bundle.

"What's that you're doing?" asked the Goat, very interested.

"Oh," said Sojo. "I'm just going to cut and collect all the grass along this path. It's the finest grass in the country, you know. And so we cut it every week and put it away."

"The finest grass, you say?" asked the Goat. "Why, I never knew that!" and he came closer to nibble along the edges of the path.

"Hi," said Sojo, and he shook his head at the goat. "That's my grass."

"Well, but look here. Can't I eat even a little of it?" asked the Goat.

"M-m. Maybe a little," said Sojo. "But you be careful not to eat too much," and he yawned and lay down under a tree. When he woke up, the Goat was gone.

But the path which Sojo was going to cut was cropped as clean as the middle of the road. Not a blade of grass was in sight. Sojo went home, yawning, to his Mammy.

And she certainly was surprised to see how well her path had been cut.

Next morning Sojo's Mammy called him to get up and go fishing. She said, "Bring me a lot of fish for my dinner. Because I like fish." And that, if you haven't guessed it, was on a Friday morning.

Sojo rubbed his eyes and ate his breakfast. He took his fishing lines and his fishing rods and went down to the river. He stuck his fishing rods in the ground and put bait on his hooks and threw the lines into the river.

Then he sat down under a tree, and pretty soon he rolled over and began to finish his sleep.

When he woke up, he saw a huge bird a-sitting on a sandbar in the middle of the river catching fish. The huge bird had a big fish-basket of skin right underneath his beak; and every time he caught a fish, he'd pop it into the basket.

Sojo sat up and wriggled his fish lines. But there was nothing on any of them. Not one single, solitary fish.

Then he yawned and called out to the huge bird, "Hi, Pelican! Good fishing?"

"Splendid!" said the Pelican, tossing a fish into the air and catching it in his fish-basket beak. "Too good, in fact."

"How's that?" asked Sojo.

"Well, you see," the Pelican shifted his weight from one great flat foot to the other great flat foot, "I've eaten all I can hold, and my basket is full, and still I keep on catching fish. But if I put them back into the water, they'll swim away and warn the others about me so I won't be able to catch any tomorrow."

"Well," said Sojo, "you're a friend of mine. Perhaps I can manage to help you out and take some of those fish off your hands. That is—off your beak. Just, of course, as a very special favor."

"Oh, would you?" asked the Pelican, very pleased.

And Sojo could. And he would. And he did. He took two catfish and a dogfish, some mudfish and three eels. And he put them all on a stick together and went home, yawning, to his Mammy.

And his Mammy certainly was surprised to see all the fish he had brought home.

Next morning Sojo's Mammy said, "It's a nice warm

day, so take the hammock and go out and rest under a tree. I've never known you to work so hard." And that, if you haven't guessed it, was on a Saturday.

So Sojo took his hammock and went out and sat under a tree. Overhead was a little red Bird sitting on a branch.

"Hi, little red Bird!" said Sojo. "Sing me a song."

The little red Bird broke into a string of notes, then cocked his head on one side. "How's that?" he asked eagerly.

"Well enough," said Sojo, yawning politely behind his hand. "Sing some more."

So the little red Bird sang some more notes. "How's that?" he asked again, cocking his head on one side.

"It's good," Sojo nodded. "But since you ask me, I think it's too short. A really good song lasts a long time. It goes on and on and on. I'm afraid you couldn't sing a real song."

"I could, too," said the little red Bird crossly; and he settled down on his branch to sing a long time.

Sojo yawned and got up to tie one end of his hammock to the tree. But the rope wasn't long enough to reach to the next tree. So he sat down again.

Pretty soon he opened his eyes and saw two bright black eyes shining in the grass. It was a very short pie-bald Python—oh, a very short one, and ab-so-lute-ly harmless.

"Look here, Sojo," whispered the very short piebald Python in a very secret piebald Python whisper. "You've given games to all the other animals. What's the matter with making up a game for me?"

"There's only one game left," said Sojo. "And you're much too small to play it," and he closed his eyes again.

"Oh, pu-please, Sojo!" begged the very small piebald Python, stretching himself to his very fullest piebald Python length. "Pu-pu-pu-pl-eee-ease!"

"Oh, all right," agreed Sojo kindly. "But I wouldn't bother with this for anyone else, because I really do need sleep." And he got up and stretched out the hammock as near as it would go to the second tree.

"Now, here's the idea. You climb that tree, so. And loop yourself through the end of the hammock, so. And catch your tail between your teeth. Now you pull and stretch, pull and stretch. And if you stop, you lose a point. But if you drop the hammock"—and Sojo looked anxious—"you lose the game. See?"

"I see," said the very short piebald Python with his mouth full of very short Python tail. "And what happens next?"

"Well, I wouldn't do it for any of the others, because I really do need sleep," said Sojo, politely yawning behind his hand. "But I'll climb into the hammock. Like this. And keep pressing downward with my back. Like this. And help you to stretch and grow."

And when Sojo's Mammy came out to see if he was resting, she found the little red Bird still singing overhead. And Sojo in the hammock was getting lots of rest. She certainly was surprised to see how well he was doing.

*By Erick Berry*

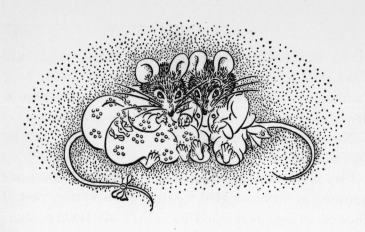

## GEORGE AND ANGELA

ONCE UPON A TIME there was a little mouse and she had seven children. They were Seraphine, Gertrude and Angela, Albert, Edward, Henry and George—and George was a bit of a pickle.

Every evening, when Cook had shut up for the night and Puss was safely away down the garden, the little mouse and her family would creep out of the hole in the larder floor, which was their home, to spend the night feeding and playing.

There was always plenty to eat, for, as the little mouse used to say, while she handed round morsels of cheese, juicy lettuce leaves or nice crusty bits of bread, "Cook is such a thoughtful woman!"

When they had eaten enough, they would rush around the larder, sliding down anything sliddery, chasing each other round the bottles and tins and learning to take cheese out of a trap without getting caught.

They had a merry time, feeding and playing, till the larder grew gray in the morning light, when the little mouse would call, "Bedtime! Come along, children!" Then they all hurried down the hole in the larder floor (which was their home), before Cook came down to her work and Puss was let in from the garden.

Now George didn't like going to bed—I told you he was a bit of a pickle.

"It's always the same," he complained to Angela one morning as they snuggled together in their cozy nest of chewed string, paper and hair, "it's always the same, just when things are getting really interesting—BED-TIME!" He leaned forward and whispered in Angela's ear, "I'm going to stay out tomorrow—and *so are you!*"

"Oo-er!" said Angela (she was never *very* original).

The next morning when the first rays of the sun peeped through the larder window the little mouse began to collect her family as usual.

"Albert!" called the little mouse, sitting up on her tail, the better to see what they were all doing.

Albert stopped admiring his whiskers in the polished surface of the tea caddy and hurried to his mother.

"Edward!"

Edward slid gracefully down the meat cover and landed at the little mouse's feet.

"Seraphine! Gertrude!"

Seraphine and Gertrude, who were skipping with their tails, ran up together.

Angela slipped behind the milk jug.

"Henry!" called the little mouse.

Henry, who was partial to onions, scuttled out from under the vegetables.

"Angela! George!"

Angela squeezed still tighter behind the milk jug, and George (who *was* a bit of a pickle) crouched under a fine new Dutch cheese the mice had only started that night.

The larder grew lighter.

"Angela! George!" cried the little mouse anxiously. "Dear, dear, where can those children be?"

Albert, Edward and Henry suggested that perhaps they had already gone home, so the little mouse, very worried and fidgety, hurried her family down to see.

The larder grew quiet and much lighter.

Upstairs Cook's alarm clock started ringing. Puss came silently along the garden path and sat on the steps by the milk bottles.

George slipped out from under the cheese and peeped over the edge of the plate.

"Angela!" he whispered—he *was* a pickle—"Angela, if we made the hole in this cheese a little bit bigger, we could sit inside all cozy and just eat and sleep . . . eat and sleep . . . eat and sleep . . ."

"Oo-er!" said Angela. . . . I told you she wasn't very bright.

The two little mice worked hard, nibbling and scratching and pushing the cheese away with their tiny front paws.

Cook stretched and yawned and started to dress. Puss stretched and yawned and started to wash.

The larder grew lighter and lighter. . . .

Presently the hole in the cheese was quite big, and first George and then Angela squeezed inside.

"Don't push so!" cried George.

"I'm not pushing," squeaked Angela. "It's the cheese!"

"Phoof! The cheese!" snorted George—but Angela was right.

The two fidgety little mice had started the cheese rolling and now it went, bumpety, bumpety, bumpety— off the plate, over the edge of the shelf—BUMP—right down onto the larder floor, where it settled at last— with the hole underneath!

The two little mice inside in the dark sat and blinked.

"George!" squeaked Angela. "We can't get out!"

Cook came downstairs, let Puss in from the garden, took up the milk and started her day's work.

The larder was now quite light and the larder door stood open just a crack.

Puss nosed round the kitchen till she came to the larder, where she put her nose to the crack of the door and sniffed; then, very soft and slinky, she squeezed through with her whiskers twitching.

Cook began to be busy with a broom.

Inside the cheese two little mice crouched down and shivered.

Puss fixed her eyes on the cheese and crept nearer and nearer; then she put out a velvet paw and patted it, very gently.

The cheese rocked backwards and forwards.

"Oh, George!" squeaked Angela.

George said nothing, but his eyes stuck out of his head like two little black beads.

Puss patted the cheese again, while her nose twitched greedily; the cheese rocked more and more. . . .

This looks as though the story were going to end badly; but—and, mind you, if it hadn't been for this it certainly would have—but just as Puss was remembering how delicious young mouse tasted, Cook came into the larder.

"Here! Hi!" she cried. "Whatever are you doing with my cheese? *I'll* teach you to roll my cheeses about. Shoo, Phwf. Phwft!" and Puss was chased out of the larder at the end of a broom.

The cheese rocked right over.

"Run!" squeaked George, and even Angela didn't need to be told twice.

The two little mice were out of that cheese and down the hole in the larder floor (which was their home) before you could say Jack Robinson. Though why anyone should ever *want* to say Jack Robinson I never could think.

The little mouse was very pleased to see George and Angela, but very cross when she heard what they had been doing.

"You will both go to bed early for a week," she told them severely. And I'm sure you will agree that it was no more than they deserved.

They never stayed out late again.

*By Cicely Englefield*

# THE LITTLE OLD WOMAN AND HOW
# SHE KEPT HER GEESE WARM

ONCE UPON A TIME there was a Little Old Woman. She lived in a little yellow house with a blue door and two blue window boxes. In each of the window boxes there were yellow tulips.

All around her house was a neat blue fence. Inside the fence was the Little Old Woman's soup garden. She called it a soup garden because she raised vegetables in it, to cook in her soup. She raised carrots, potatoes, turnips, garlic, cabbages, and onions.

The Little Old Woman was very poor. If she had not been so clever, she probably could not have made ends meet. But she was a great one for using her head. She always said, "What is the good of having a head if you don't use it?"

So, as you will see, she managed to get along very well.

One cold winter night the Little Old Woman was out in the barn putting her geese to bed. She gave them some corn and took off their little red coats. Then she brushed each little coat with a whisk broom and carefully shook out the wrinkles.

As she was folding the coats in a neat pile, she thought:

"My poor geese must be very cold at night. I have my cozy fire and my feather bed. But they have not even a blanket to keep them warm."

After the geese had eaten their corn, they began to go to roost.

"Honk, honk!" said the big gander, and he hopped up on the roost.

"Honk, honk!" said the gray goose, and she hopped up on the roost.

"Honk, honk!" said all the other geese, and they hopped up on the roost.

Then the Little Old Woman closed the barn door and went into the house. When she went to bed, she lay awake worrying about the geese. After a while she said to herself:

"I cannot sleep a wink for thinking how cold the geese must be. I had better bring them in the house where it is warm."

So the Little Old Woman dressed herself and went out to the barn to fetch the geese. She shooed them off the roost and put on their little red coats. She picked up two geese, and tucking one under each arm, she carried them into the house.

When the Little Old Woman had brought all the geese into the house, she said to herself:

"Now I must get them ready for bed again."

She took off their little red coats and gave the geese some corn. Then she brushed each little coat with a whisk broom and carefully shook out all the wrinkles.

As she was folding the coats in a neat pile, she thought:

"It was very clever of me to bring the geese into the house. Now they will be warm, and I shall be able to sleep."

Then the Little Old Woman undressed herself again and went to bed.

After the geese had eaten their corn, they began to roost.

"Honk, honk!" said the gander, and he hopped up on the foot of the Little Old Woman's bed.

"Honk, honk!" said the gray goose, and she hopped up on the Little Old Woman's bed.

"Honk, honk!" said all the other geese, and they tried to hop up on the foot of the Little Old Woman's bed.

But it was not a very big bed, and there was not enough room for all the geese to roost. They began to fight. They pushed and shoved each other. They hissed and squawked and flapped their wings.

All night long the geese pushed and shoved each other. All night long they hissed and squawked and flapped their wings.

They made so much noise that the Little Old Woman did not sleep a wink.

"This will never do," she said. "When they were in the barn, I did not sleep for thinking how cold they must be. When they are in the house, I cannot sleep because they make so much noise. Perhaps if I use my head I shall know what to do."

The Little Old Woman tied a wet towel around her forehead. Then she sat down with her forefinger against her nose and shut her eyes.

She used her head and used her head, and after a while she knew what to do.

"I will move the roost into the house," she said. "The geese will have the cozy fire to keep them warm. Then I will move my bed out into the barn. My feather bed will keep me warm, and I will not be worrying about the geese. They will not keep me awake with their noise. I shall sleep quite comfortably in the barn."

The Little Old Woman moved the roost into the house, and she moved her bed out into the barn.

When night came again, she brought the geese into the house. After she had fed them some corn, she took off their little red coats. Then they all hopped up on the roost, and the Little Old Woman went out to the barn to sleep.

Her feather bed kept her as warm as toast. She was not worried about the geese, because she knew that they were warm too. So she slept as sound as a top all night long.

*By Hope Newell*

## THE PONY TREE

There was once a little boy whose name was Jimmie.

He had a sister, Joan, but Joan had gone to spend a week with her grandmother!

His two dearest friends who lived right next door were Susan Sill and Nellie Nelson.

The dearest wish of these children, since the day the circus came to town, was for a pony, and a little yellow cart, and red harness—just like the clown had!

Every day Jimmie said to his Mother, "I do want a little pony. Please!"

And every day Mother said, "Darling, if I bought you a pony, I wouldn't have enough money to buy spinach and carrots and prunes for you, and shoes for you to go to school!"

So Susan and Nellie and Jimmie thought and thought about it.

Bye and bye Susan said, "Maybe, if we were good, the fairies would bring us a pony."

So the children were good. They were very good.

They ran errands for their mothers.

They knew all the answers in school!

They kept their clothes clean!

One night after they had been good three whole days, something happened!

Jimmie was lying in bed, looking up at the moon.

Suddenly, right out of the moon came a fairy!

He said, "Jimmie, you have been good, and I have brought a present for you. It is a seed. Plant it in your garden."

And the fairy flew away.

And what do you think Jimmie did?

Well, he got right out of bed in his bare feet and ran down to the garden.

And in a hole, in the middle of the lawn, Jimmie planted the seed and patted it down. Then he went back to bed.

In the morning Jimmie said, "Oh, Mother, a fairy gave me a seed and I planted it in the garden."

But Mother said, "Darling, you only dreamed it."

Sometimes Jimmie thought maybe his mother didn't believe in fairies.

Jimmie said to his father, "Father, I planted a seed that a fairy gave me, in the lawn," and his father laughed and said:

"What an imagination that child has!" And he went on shaving.

Sometimes Jimmie was sure Father didn't believe in fairies!

As soon as breakfast was over Jimmie went out and told Susan and Nellie all about it—and weren't they glad!

They all ran to the garden and there—what do you suppose?

Right out of the ground where Jimmie had planted the seed a plant was growing.

Mother said, "It is a weed, you must pull it up right away. Father won't like it!"

But the children begged so hard that finally she said they might leave it. And she sent them all to school.

But in school, oh my! Susan could not keep her mind on her lessons!

She looked out of the window and thought of the Fairy Seed.

She did not hear the teacher! It was all quite, quite dreadful!

The moment school was out, Susan and Jimmie and Nellie raced for home, and—what do you think? The plant had grown into a tree, and it had three blossoms on it!

The children stood and looked and looked.

Even Mother was surprised.

The children did not want to go in to lunch, and so Jimmie's mother gave them three bowls of bread and milk under the tree.

Pretty soon in the center of each flower they could see something forming. At first there were just two little points, but very soon they knew that they were—ears!

Then they saw that the ears were attached to something. It was a tiny pony head!

And then it was school time. The children wept but they had to go.

That afternoon Jimmie was so naughty that the teacher had to make him stand in the corner.

And when the teacher asked Susan to spell "kitten," Susan said, "P-o-n-y."

After school, they thought they would never get home!

Their feet were so heavy.

But when they got there—what do you think?

From each blossom was growing a pony! And from between the leaves on the tree were growing little yellow wagons and red harnesses!

Just think!

Jimmie cried, "Oh, Mother, may I pick a pony?"

Mother looked worried and said, "Oh, I'm afraid they aren't ripe yet. It would be very bad to pick a pony before it is ripe."

So the children waited and it was well they did, for as each pony grew larger it grew heavier, and bent down its branch more and more until finally its feet touched the ground.

Nellie had called in the other children from the block.

And now they were all standing around watching.

So Susan picked a black pony, and he seemed very glad to see her and licked her face!

Nellie picked a white pony, and kissed him on the nose.

And Jimmie picked a brown pony and hugged him.

The children harnessed the ponies to the carts and gave all the children rides, up and down the street.

And after that, I guess those fathers and mothers believed in fairies!

*By Charlotte Brate*

## THE THREE ELEVATORS

THERE WAS ONE immense building in the City o' Ligg; it was twenty-seven stories high! At the end of the main corridor, which was a gorgeous affair, paved with marble and walled with malachite, there was a shaft, in which lived three elevators.

One of these elevators was very, very strong. One was very, very swift. One was neither very strong nor very swift, but it made up for it by being very, very clever, as you shall see.

The strong elevator was used chiefly for carrying up heavy pieces of merchandise, and was not fitted up so beautifully as the others. The swift one was an "Express Elevator," and did not stop till he got to the twentieth story. If you wanted to go to a floor between that and the ground floor, you had to take the one in the middle of the three, which was the clever elevator.

At night, after the power was turned off, the three elevators rested, side by side on the ground floor, at the end of the corridor. It was then that they used to gossip over the day's work, and the strong one would brag of the heavy cases he had lifted; the swift one would boast of how he had made the trip to the roof in two minutes many and many a time, and could do it in 1:46, if necessary, with a good elevator boy; and the clever one did not say much, but she would lead the others on, and keep them talking.

One day the swift elevator, who always made the last trip, dropped down to the floor, as the electric lights were turned off, in great excitement.

"What do you think?" he said. "A great, stupid house has crawled on top of this building; it is a ten-story house, too!"

"Heavens! Do you suppose we'll have to make thirty-seven-story trips now? That is too much of a good thing!" said the strong elevator.

"I am afraid we shall," said the clever one, "unless we can do something about it, in a hurry!"

"What can we do?" cried the other two.

"Well," said the clever one to the swift one, "if you could only go fast enough—"

"Oh, no fear, *I* can go fast enough; you wait!" said the swift elevator, shaking her annunciator drops.

"Or if you were a little stronger," continued the one in the center, as she looked slyly at the heavy freight car.

The strong one rattled his rope with his chuckles.

"Well, I think you can trust *me!*"

"Well, then, perhaps we can do it," said the clever little elevator.

"But *how?*" inquired the other two.

"Why, it's only necessary to push the house off; and it doesn't matter whether you shoot up fast and knock it off with a jerk, or go up slowly—the way old freightie does—and push it off by main force; it's all the same, as long as the house falls off. I'm not very strong, and I'm not very swift, but I can see the way it ought to be done, easily enough."

Then the other two consulted together. "Let *me* try first!" said one, and "No, let *me* try first," said the other, till they had to appeal to the middle one to decide which should have the honor of the first trial.

"Let the express go first," said the clever one, "and if he can't do it, then the goods elevator may try it."

So the express elevator drew a long breath and braced himself against a floor. *"Go!"* cried the others. He shot up like a bullet out of a gun, so fast and so hard that he drove up and up, right into the house on top of the building, where there was no shaft, and tore a hole, ten stories high, clear through it. But his speed was so great that he flew through the house, high into the air, and then fell down, *smash!* on the roof of the house, and was killed.

"Now, it is your turn," said the clever one, smiling wickedly.

The strong freight car took a tight hold on his rope, and crawled slowly up, story by story, till he had reached the top of the shaft, at the twenty-seventh floor. There he rested a few minutes to get his breath. Then he put his head against the house, and exerted all his strength in a mighty effort. He pushed and pushed; but though he lifted the whole house up about twenty feet, he could do no more.

Then he shouted down the shaft to the other: "Come on and help! It's heavier than I thought, and I can't hold it much longer! Come quickly!"

"I'm right here!" said the clever elevator, who had stolen up the shaft after him. "I'll help."

But instead of helping, that sly little car crawled out of the hole the swift elevator had made, and crept along the roof of the building in the space left by the other's holding up the house. It was lucky for her that the stupid freight elevator could not see; for if he had dropped the house, it would have crushed her flatter than a pancake. She was a little frightened, but she got safely to the edge, and dropped to a roof near by, and lay there laughing to her own naughty little self.

The strong elevator held up the house as long as he could, and then let it drop with a groan.

"Why didn't you push more?" he said. But when he came down and found that the clever one was gone, he didn't know what to make of it at all. He was a very dull machine, and he never knew what a fool the sly one had made of them both.

But the clever little car stayed up on the roof in the sun watching the lively City o' Ligg all day, and slept all night, thanking her ropes that she didn't have to work any more, and didn't have to obey an ignorant elevator boy who would stop her with a jerk, and start her with a jounce. And unless she has been taken away and made into a streetcar, she is there yet!

*By Gelett Burgess*

# A HAPPY CHRISTMAS TREE

AN EVERGREEN TREE grew in the front yard near the porch of a large farmhouse. Every Christmas it was decorated with gay colored lights. They shone in the farm windows at night. They sparkled and danced across the lawn for people who passed by to see. Everyone thought the little Tree was very beautiful. But he was not happy. He wanted to be loaded from top to bottom with Christmas gifts like the Christmas tree inside the window of the big house.

"Twinkling lights are not enough," the Evergreen Tree said. "I am not a real Christmas Tree with real Christmas gifts. I am only a pretend."

Then a bright idea flashed into the small Tree's mind. "If I could only travel—I could see the way with my gay lights," he said. "Then I might find some Christmas toys to put on my branches."

Suddenly something happened—

There was a terrific sound—

Rumble. . . .

Rumble. . . .

Rumbling. . . .

Something shook the earth very hard. Then it shook the earth gently. Then very hard again! There was a rushing sound of wind. The big farmhouse rattled its windows. The Snow Man in the path near the house shivered and shook. He shook until—

he lost his hat—

he lost the pipe out of his mouth—

he lost his coal buttons.

And the small Evergreen Tree shook! He shook until his gay Christmas lights blinked—

and blinked—

and blinked.

"Oo—oo—oo—" went the wind blowing around the Evergreen Tree. It tore at his branches. It pushed and pulled. It tugged at his roots. It blew snow all over him.

"What—is—happening? What—is—happening—to me?" called out the small Evergreen Tree.

"Why, it's an earthquake," shouted the Snow Man. "Look out there. Hold on tight. You are moving."

"I can't hold on," said the Tree. "I never—moved— before in my life."

"Well, you're moving now," replied the Snow Man.

And sure enough. Out of the snow came the roots of

the little Evergreen Tree and he was off! He caught his breath. Then he was glad. "I—am—to—have—my —wish," he called to the Snow Man and started out of the yard.

"Merry Christmas to you," shouted the Snow Man as he shivered and shook in the path near the big house.

"Merry Christmas," shouted back the Tree, almost out of breath.

Twinkle, twinkle, twinkle
     and
          Jingle, jingle, jingle,
went his lights as down, down the road went the Evergreen Tree. Faster and faster behind him blew the wind.

Soon the Tree was out of sight of the big farmhouse and the Snow Man.

"Oo—oo—oo—" cried the wind.

Tramp, tramp, tramp,
     Jingle, jingle, jingle
          and
               Twinkle, twinkle, twinkle,
went the Evergreen Tree.

On and on he went right down through the middle of the road. At last the wind pushed him up to a Store on the edge of the town. There were many, many toys in the Store window, so—

With all his gay lights twinkling, the Evergreen Tree opened the door of the Store and rushed in.

"Store," called out the Evergreen Tree, "will you give me some of your toys to make me a real Christmas Tree?"

"Well, I might let you have some, for I can't sell any more before Christmas. But where did you come from?" replied the Store.

"It's a long story," answered the Tree. "Every year at Christmas time, I have been shining in the yard of a big farmhouse, and every year I have wanted presents hanging on my branches for children. But this year something strange happened. Didn't you feel the earthquake?"

"I certainly did," said the Store. "All my toys came tumbling and dancing off my shelves in a hurry."

"Well, that is how I got here. The earthquake started me off," said the Evergreen Tree.

Then the Store began to take toys down from his shelf. He even tied them on the Tree. And soon a drum, a Teddy Bear, a rocking horse, two dolls, a doll carriage and some picture books were hanging from the branches of the Evergreen Tree.

"Thank you, Store," said the Evergreen Tree. "Now I feel like a real Christmas Tree!" And out of the Store the Tree danced down the roadway to the other end of the town.

There stood a house among some trees and it was very dark. Not a candle gleamed in any one of its windows. The Evergreen Tree walked up to the door and knocked.

"Woof—woof! Woof—woof!" barked a little dog. "What do you want at this hour of the night?"

"I am a Christmas Tree," said the voice outside, "May I come in?"

The little dog opened the door very quickly.

"Have you any dog biscuit on your branches?" he asked.

"I am sorry," said the Evergreen Tree. "I never thought of dog biscuit. But I do have oranges and candy."

"I never eat them," said the little dog. "Have you any bones?"

"I never thought of bones, either," replied the Tree. "But I have

> a doll,
>> a Teddy Bear,
>>> a drum,
>>>> and a rocking horse!"

"Well, I don't play with toys," barked the little dog. "You had better try another house." And with a snort he pushed the door shut.

The Evergreen Tree went on down the road. The toys rattled and rattled against his branches. His gay lights flickered and sparkled.

By and by he came to another house. It was very dark but the Tree could see smoke curling out of its chimney.

"I'll try this house," the Tree said to himself. So he walked up to the door and knocked.

"Miew! Miew! Miew!" came a faint voice from within. A pussy cat inside stretched herself before the fire and came to the door.

"What do you want at this hour of the night?" asked the pussy cat crossly.

"I am a Christmas Tree," said the voice outside.

The pussy cat opened the door very quickly. "Have you any pink mice on your branches?" she inquired.

"I am sorry," said the Evergreen Tree, "I haven't any, but I have oranges and candy."

"Well, I never eat them. Haven't you any catnip balls?"

"Catnip balls! I never thought of catnip balls, but I have

a Teddy Bear,

a drum,

and a rocking horse."

"Well, those toys are not for me. They must be for some boy or girl." Then the pussy shut the door. She yawned and went back to stretch herself out again in front of the fire.

So the Evergreen Tree walked on. And he walked and he walked until he came to another house. It was a very dark house, but one tiny candle shone through the window. Surely, he thought, there must be boys and girls living here.

So he walked up to the door and knocked.

Now in this house there lived a little old man and a little old lady. They had been sitting by the fire and wishing they had some Christmas toys for their grandchildren. But they were very poor and couldn't buy any. And while they were sitting there wishing, they had fallen asleep.

The little old man was snoring loudly. Snore! snore!

The little old lady was snoring gently. Snore! snore!

The Evergreen Tree knocked again, louder this time—

Knock!

Knock!

Knock!

The little old lady woke up with a start. She poked the little old man.

"Somebody is knocking at the door," she said. "Who can it be at this hour of the night?"

The little old man opened the door quickly. In walked the Tree, his lights gleaming and his toys rattling and jingling.

"Where did you come from?" asked the little old lady.

"Well, it's a long story," answered the Tree. "But that earthquake started me off and here I am. Do you know any boys and girls who need Christmas presents?"

At this the little old lady clapped her hands for joy. "Oh, I do—I do! Our grandchildren, Nancy and Charles, live next door," she said. "We have been wishing for a tree for them but we have no money to buy one."

"Thank you," said the Tree, as he went out of the door, "I'll hurry over." Across the snow the Tree went to the next door. He didn't stop even to knock. He walked straight in and stood himself up in a corner.

Then he gave himself a gentle shake to straighten out the toys that had tangled up in his branches.

Jingle, jingle, tingled the toys.

Blink, blink, blink, went the Evergreen Tree's lights.

The Evergreen Tree stood very still. His lights shone on the clock on the mantel. They were sleepy.

Twinkle, twinkle, twinkle!

Blink, blink, blink, nodded the lights.

The clock struck one—two—three. There was not a sound in the house.

The clock struck four. Still there was not a sound in the house.

The clock struck five.

Surely someone will wake up soon, thought the Evergreen Tree. It's time to build the fires so the house will be warm.

Then the clock struck six.

A stair creaked, then another—

Creak! Creak! they went.

Someone was up. The Christmas Tree waited.

Creak-crack!

Creak-crack!

Footsteps came down, down the stairs, nearer and nearer.

Father hurried into the room and over to the big stove. He built a crackling fire. Then he hurried out of the room. He did not see the Christmas Tree.

The stairs creaked—

Creak-crack!

Creak-crack!

Mother hurried into the room. She laid some clothes on chairs near the stove so they would be warm for Nancy and Charles. Then she hurried out to the kitchen. She did not see the Christmas Tree, either.

Again the stairs creaked—

Creak-crack!

Creak-crack!

The children are coming now, thought the Tree as

he stood very straight and still. The footsteps came nearer. The stair door opened. There stood Nancy and Charles in their pajamas.

Nancy ran shivering over to the big iron stove.

Charles ran after her.

"Here are our clothes," said Nancy. "Mother has them warming for us by the fire."

They sat down on the bench to put on their clothes. They stretched their toes out toward the crackling fire.

"Oh, look!" said Nancy, "we have new stockings."

"There is something big and round in mine," exclaimed Charles.

"There is something big and round in mine, too," exclaimed Nancy.

"It's a big, red apple," laughed Charles.

"It's a big, red apple," laughed Nancy.

("Wait until they see me," chuckled the Tree to himself.)

Nancy and Charles reached for their shoes.

"There is a stick of candy in my shoe," sang out Nancy.

"There is a stick of candy in my shoe, too," sang out Charles.

("Wait until they see me!" chuckled the Tree to himself again.)

"Maybe there is something in my coat pocket," shouted Charles. He put his hand in but there was nothing there.

"I'll look in my apron pocket," exclaimed Nancy. But when she put her hand in, it came out empty.

("Now is the time," chuckled the Tree. "I'll shake myself.") And he did.

Rattle! Rattle! Rattle!
went all the Tree's toys.

Jingle! Jingle! Jingle!
went all his bells.

Twinkle! Twinkle! Twinkle!
went all his lights together.

Nancy caught Charles by the arm. She held on tight to him. They looked at each other. They looked at the Tree. For a minute they could not speak at all. Then they ran toward the gay lights. They danced around the Tree shouting—

"A Christmas Tree!

A Christmas Tree!

A really, truly Christmas Tree."

Mother heard the children shouting. Father heard them shouting, too. They came running in from the kitchen. They saw the children dancing around the Tree. They could hardly believe their eyes.

Father caught Charles up in his arms and danced around the Tree. Nancy ran to her mother.

"Mother! Mother!" she cried. "Come dance with me." And round and round the Tree they danced together.

Suddenly the door opened. Grandma and Grandpa walked in.

"Come and dance with us!" shouted Charles.

"Come and dance with us!" shouted Nancy.

And they all danced around the Christmas Tree—

Grandfather, Grandmother, Father, Mother, Nancy and Charles.

But the happiest time of all for the Evergreen Tree was when the children took off their presents. Then it was that he knew that he was a real Christmas Tree at last.

There were the two dolls and the doll carriage for Nancy . . . the drum, the Teddy Bear, and the rocking horse for Charles . . . and bright colored picture books for both.

"Dear me," said the Christmas Tree to himself, "I have liked Christmas always but I have never had such a happy Christmas before in all my life."

*By Frances Anne Brown*

## GISSING AND THE TELEPHONE

IN THE HOUSE where Gissing lived there was a speaking tube in the hall upstairs. This speaking tube was a great joy. When children blew in it it made a loud whistling squeal down in the kitchen. Done suddenly, it often startled cooks and cats half out of their wits. It sounded like the squeak of a mouse as big as a police dog. But like many amusing jokes this got overdone. And so, to prevent the speaking tube becoming a nuisance, it was agreed that it was a private magic telephone to Santa Claus, and must not be used except in the week before Christmas. Santa Claus, like everyone else, does not care to be bothered with unnecessary telephone calls. Like many other wise people he does not allow his number to be listed in the book, and only tells it to his intimate friends.

But, of course, in the week before Christmas everyone is so busy that a little extra squeaking in the kitchen does not matter.

Now Gissing, arriving in the house as a very small puppy, heard so much about this Santa Claus telephone that he really believed it. He heard the children making their plans, and writing out lists, and then blowing in the mouthpiece until it squawked, and announcing down the tube their desires for Christmas. He wished very much that he, too, could telephone to Santa Claus and tell what he wanted. But he felt bashful about doing it, and a little ashamed because he did not understand very well just what Christmas was. He heard all the children talking about it, and he tried to pick up some information by listening, but he did not learn anything definite. You know how it is: when everyone else seems to know about something that you yourself don't understand, you don't like to admit your ignorance. You listen carefully, hoping you'll overhear some remark that will explain what it's all about.

Gissing spoke in a casual way to the others, hoping to lead them into saying something that would help him to know what was going to happen. He would say, "Christmas will be fun, won't it!" or some such innocent thing. But their replies, though enthusiastic, did not help much. In his heart he was lonely because he felt there was some great secret that they knew and he didn't. "Oh, I wish someone would tell me what Christmas is," he said to himself. "Is it something to eat? Is it something to wear? Is it a game? Is it a person? And who is this mysterious Santa Claus?"

One day so much happened that Gissing felt more sure than ever that Christmas was going to be something very important. It was even a little frightening. From early morning the house was full of movement and hullabaloo. Tin horns were blown, there was a crackling of paper parcels being unwrapped, and the living room was so crowded with children playing with new toys that he retired under the dining-room table. Even there he was not safe, for by chance he squatted on the electric bell, and after many visits made to the front door he was found and moved off. There were smells of balsam and evergreen, and a whiff of brandy from the kitchen. Most alarming of all, the pudding caught fire and was carried in blazing. It was all very puzzling to a puppy, and Gissing lay under the couch feeling wistful. Everyone seemed too occupied to play with him, and he began to think that it was all because he had never talked into the magic telephone.

After supper things quieted down a bit. The children were got to bed early. The grown-ups, exhausted by picking up so much paper and string, sat down to rest. Gissing saw his chance. With great labor he pulled his toy box into the upstairs hall and stood on it so he could reach the speaking tube. He blew into it, and heard it squeal at the other end. Then he said, just as he had heard the children do, "Give me North Pole 1." To his great surprise he heard a deep voice coming back to him through the tube. "Santa Claus speaking," it said.

Santa Claus had had a long day. He had just got home, very tired after delivering toys all over the world. He was so tired that even before putting away the sleigh and the reindeer he had come into his house to sit down for a few moments and smoke a pipe. Everything was ready for a quiet evening. His slippers were warming in front of the fire; on the mantel a thermos jug of hot cocoa was waiting for him. He had left the door open to remind himself that he still had to go out and stable his reindeer for the night.

Santa was a little annoyed when the telephone rang. He believed that he had earned his ease. He was intending to rest his feet a bit, and then, with a happy feeling, he was going to tear off the 25 on the calendar pad that hung on the wall.

"Who is it?" he asked.

"This is Gissing," said a small and rather frightened voice that sounded very far away. "You know, Gissing in the Roslyn Estates. At Mr. Mistletoe's house."

Of course Santa knew about the Roslyn Estates, but he had never heard about Gissing, who was still so young that his name had not been entered on the lists. Santa gets the names and addresses of all the dogs from the Town Hall in Manhasset, where the dog licenses are registered. However, he answered very kindly.

"Yes, Gissing," he said. "How are you?"

"Well, I'm fine," said Gissing, "but I thought I'd better tell you what I want for Christmas."

It was on the tip of Santa's tongue to say, a little crossly, "But Christmas is over. You're too late." But he could guess from the trembly sound of Gissing's voice that there must be some misunderstanding.

"All right, Gissing," he said in an encouraging voice. "What is it?"

"What have you got?" asked Gissing eagerly.

Santa Claus almost laughed. Gissing, even when he was a small puppy, was always rather impudent. Santa looked at his shelves. There were only a few toys remaining, now that all that year's Christmas presents had been delivered.

"Well," said Santa patiently, "I have a toy schooner, a train, a doll, a rubber ball, a rake, a pail and shovel, a football, a white china cat, a paint-box, and a toy automobile."

Gissing was so excited he could hardly hold all those ideas in his head.

"Would you mind, please, repeating the list?" he asked politely.

Santa repeated, smiling to himself.

"I think I would like a white china cat," said Gissing. He wanted very much to ask for the toy automobile also, but he restrained himself.

Santa Claus sighed at the thought of going all the way back to the Roslyn Estates that night. He was rather angry at Mr. Mistletoe for not having properly instructed Gissing about Christmas and told him the date. But he did not want anyone to be disappointed.

"Very well," he said. "You hang up your stocking, and the cat will be there in the morning. Merry Christmas!"

"Here's looking at you," replied Gissing. It was a phrase he had heard the grown-ups say, and it was the only thing he could think of at the moment. He pulled his toy box back into the nursery, quietly, so that no one would know what he had been up to, got out his largest stocking, and went to bed.

Santa Claus had a cup of hot cocoa, and gave some to the reindeer, who were peevish at having to go out again. But with such a light load to carry, the sleigh sped swiftly. Across the snowy curve of the world the red sleigh went flashing. Great gauzes of daffodil yellow rippled and flickered in the dark blue, the wonderful Northern Lights. A brilliant star burned steadily right above the Pole, the North Star, the true Christmas Star. You can find it easily in the sky (unless you live south of the Equator) because the two stars in the end of the Dipper point straight to it.

It was the quietest night of the year, the night when all the children go to sleep at once because they are tired out with toys and excitements. Santa and the reindeer soon got over their irritation at having to go out again. It was very peaceful, even better than the hurry of Christmas Eve.

When Gissing woke up the next morning, there was the china cat. And not only the cat. Because Gissing's request had been so modest, Santa had brought along all the toys that were left—the schooner, the train, the doll, the ball, the rake, the pail and shovel, the football, the paint-box, and the aunbile.

It wasn't until Gissing was much older that he learned that Santa Claus had made a special trip, all the way from the North Pole to the Roslyn Estates. And that was why Gissing himself, when he grew up and went on a long adventure, was careful to get home on Christmas Eve, so that his puppies wouldn't be disappointed.

*By Christopher Morley*

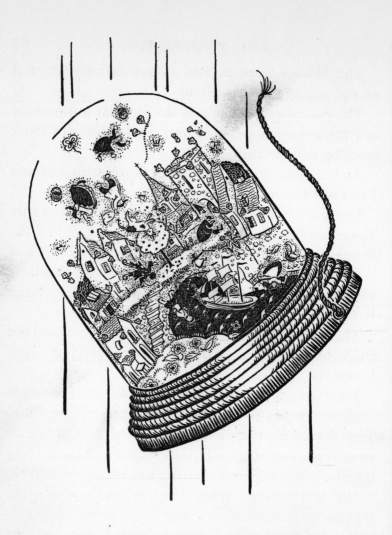

## THE MUSICAL BOX

ONCE UPON A TIME there was a very happy Little
French Town. It was so happy that it did not mind
being kept in a Glass Case. In fact, it was glad, for no
Dust could get at it and the People's Clothes were always bright in color.

The Houses were painted in gay colors—red, and orange and green and yellow.

The Sun always shone and the Sky was always blue and there were big Blue Flowers on the River Bank near the Sailing Ship.

And a beautiful little Cherry Tree with crimson Fruit was planted halfway across the Bridge.

Every day Somebody pulled a String under the Little Town and then the Bells of the Town rang and all the People crossed the Bridge. There are some People you are sure to see—there's the Miller with his Sack of Flour and the Women going to Market with large Baskets on their arms.

There's the Blind Beggar and his Black Dog; and the Priest hurrying to the Church, always carrying a Red Umbrella.

Look over the Bridge and you'll see the Laundress washing clothes in the River near the Sailing Ship. The Waves are very white. And then, of course, we were forgetting the Little Girl with the Pail, driving the black and white Cow in front of her, to be milked.

It's such a happy Little Town when the Bells ring that one wishes one were living there oneself.

But one day a fearful thing happened. Someone forgot to pull the String, and so the Bells could not ring and the People could not cross the Bridge.

For months the People waited, but always in vain.

It was terrible. NOBODY COULD MOVE!

The Miller stood by the crooked Steps near the Bridge with his Sack on his shoulder. "Oh, dear," he groaned, "I'm getting old. This Sack gets heavier and heavier. My shoulders ache till I would drop—if I only could!

"BUT I CANNOT MOVE!"

The Women were going to Market. They had Ducks to buy and Cheeses and Salad and Wine. "Oh, dear," they sighed. "We shall be late. All the best things will have gone. Come, let's hurry!"

BUT THEY COULDN'T MOVE!

The Blind Beggar shouted to his Black Dog. "Here, Tootoo, move along, can't you! If we're not at the Church Door before the Wedding Party there'll be no bone for you tonight."

But Tootoo's nose was glued to a stone.

The Priest tried to hurry across the Bridge to the Church, but his feet would not pass the patch of Dandelions by his right boot. He read the marriage service to the Dandelions, but could go no further.

IT WAS VERY STRANGE!

And then, of course, there was the Soldier on the Fort. His duty was to walk round and round, and if he could look down and watch the Laundress he was happy. But for months he had not seen her. He stood with his back to her.

AND HE COULD NOT MOVE!

For Months the Little Town in the Glass Case was left on the Shelf. And nobody came, until . . .

One morning Somebody was careless
    and
      it
        fell
          down!

In the Little Town there was a terrible Thunderstorm. First the Earth shook and then it rocked. Windows were flung open and smashed. Loud Rumbles were
heard from the River. The Ship trembled and began to
toss. The People shivered with fear. The Earth shook
and rocked more. But the worst was yet to come. . . .
The whole Town was flung into Space and hurled
down
    and down
        and down.

The Little Girl left her Cow and jumped over the
Bridge into the Ship, while the Soldier on the Fort was
carried down through the air to the Riverside—where
he fainted among the Blue Flowers.

As for the Market Women, they got so muddled up
with their Baskets and their Petticoats that they forgot
all about the marketing.

But then a wonderful thing happened. The Bells of
the Town began to peal, louder and louder, till they
filled the whole place with Music and Joy.

They filled the People with Joy, too, so that they forgot the terrible Earthquake and laughed and moved.

The Priest took one leap forward right over the Dandelions with his Red Umbrella in the air.

The Miller flung his Sack away and danced and sang.

The Blind Beggar's Dog ran off and stole a Duck
from the Market Place, while the Soldier, when he re-
covered, found himself beside the Laundress. They
were so happy and the Blue Flowers opened and grew
tall to look at them!

And then what happened?

Somebody heard the Music and saw the Little Town
in the Glass Case lying on the Floor and put it back on
the Shelf.

And after that,
Every day,
They pulled the String
That made the Music;
And the People walked across the Bridge
And Everybody lived happily ever after.

### THE MORAL

Now you know the sort of thing
That will befall a Little Town
If you forget to pull the String
Or let the Box come tumbling down.
Even the Heavenly Stars may fail
And Lilies sulk beneath the ground,
Learn then the Moral of this Tale:
'TIS MUSIC MAKES THE WORLD GO ROUND!

*By Clare Leighton*

## THE OGRE THAT PLAYED JACKSTRAWS

ONCE THERE WAS a terrible giant ogre, and he lived in a huge castle that was built right in the middle of a valley. All men had to pass by it when they came to the king's palace on the rock at the head of the valley. And they were all terribly afraid of the ogre, and ran just as fast as they could when they went by. And when they looked back as they were running, they could see the ogre sitting on the wall of his castle. And he scowled at them so fiercely that they ran as fast as ever they could. For the ogre had a head as large as a barrel, and great black eyes sunk deep under long bushy eyelashes. And when he opened his mouth, they saw it was full of teeth; and so they ran away faster than ever, without caring to see any more.

And the king wanted to get rid of the ogre, and he sent his men to drive the ogre away and to tear down his castle. But the ogre scowled at them so savagely that their teeth began to fall out, and they all turned back and said they dare not fight such a horrid creature. Then Roger, the king's son, rode his black horse Hurricane up against the door of the ogre's castle, and struck hard against it with his iron glove. Then the door opened and the ogre came out and seized Roger in one hand and the great black horse in the other and rubbed their heads together, and while he did this he made them very small. Then he tumbled them over the wall into the ogre's garden. And they crawled through a hole in the garden fence and both ran home, Roger one way and Hurricane the other; and neither dared tell the king nor anyone else where he had been, nor what the ogre had done to him. But it was two or three days before they became large again.

Then the king sent out some men with a cannon to batter down the walls of the ogre's castle. But the ogre sat on the wall and caught the cannon balls in his hand and tossed them back at the cannon, so that they broke the wheels and scared away all the men. And when the cannon sounded, the ogre roared so loudly that all the windows in the king's palace were broken, and the queen and all the princesses went down in the cellar and hid among the sugar barrels, and stuffed cotton in their ears till the noise should stop. And whatever the king's men tried to do, the ogre made it worse and worse.

And at last no one dared to go out into the valley beside the ogre's castle, and no one dared look at it from anywhere, because when the ogre scowled all who saw him dropped to the ground with fear, and their teeth began to fall out, and when the ogre roared there was no one who could bear to hear it.

So the king and all his men hid in the cellar of the castle with the queen and the princesses, and they stuffed their ears full of cotton, and the ogre scowled and roared and had his own way.

But there was one little boy named Pennyroyal, who tended the black horse Hurricane; and he was not afraid of anything, because he was a little boy. And the little boy said he would go out and see the ogre and tell him to go away. And they were all so scared that they could not ask him not to go. So Pennyroyal put on his hat, filled his pocket with marbles and took his kite under his arm, and went down the valley to the castle of the ogre. The ogre sat on the wall and looked at him, but the little boy was not afraid, and so it did the ogre no good to scowl. Then Pennyroyal knocked on the ogre's door, and the ogre opened it and looked at the little boy.

"Please, Mr. Ogre, may I come in?" said Pennyroyal; and the ogre opened the door, and the little boy began to walk around the castle looking at all the things. There was one room filled with bones, but the ogre was ashamed of it, and did not want to let the little boy see it. So when Pennyroyal was not looking, the ogre just changed the room and made it small—so that instead of a room full of bones it became just a box of jackstraws. And the big elephant he had there to play with he made into a lap-elephant, and the little boy took it in his hand and stroked its tiny tusks and tied a knot in its trunk.

And everything that could frighten the little boy the ogre made small and pretty, so that they had great times together.

And by and by the ogre grew smaller and smaller, and took off his ugly old face with the long teeth and bushy eyebrows and dropped them on the floor and covered them with a wolf-skin. Then he sat down on the wolf-skin and the little boy sat down on the floor beside him, and they began to play jackstraws with the box of jackstraws that had been a room full of bones. The ogre had never been a boy himself, so jackstraws was the only game he knew how to play. Then the elephant he had made small snuggled down between them on the floor. And as they played with each other, the castle itself grew small, and shrank away until there was just room enough for them and their game.

Up in the palace, when the ogre stopped roaring, the king's men looked out and saw that the ogre's castle was gone. Then Roger, the king's son, called for Pennyroyal. But when he could not find the boy, he saddled the black horse Hurricane himself and rode down the valley to where the ogre's castle had been. When he came back he told the king that the ogre and his castle were all gone. Where the castle stood there was nothing left but a board tent under the oak tree, and in the tent there were just two little boys playing jackstraws, and between them on the ground lay a candy elephant.

That was all. For the terrible ogre was one of that kind of ogres that will do to folks just what folks do to him. There isn't any other kind of ogre.

*By David Starr Jordan*

## THE THREE APPLES

EVERY SUMMER the apple tree which grew in the Old
Apple Woman's garden was covered thickly with
apples; and as the summer days passed, these apples
grew big and red and ripe, and at last fell one by one
to the ground. Then the Apple Woman would come
out and gather them up, and store them away until the
time came when she could carry them to the fair and
sell them.

But once, when the Old Apple Woman thought that
all her apples were safely stored away, she went out to

have a last look at her tree, and there she saw, right at the very tip-top, round and red against the sky, three apples still remaining. The Old Apple Woman stood and looked at them, and she saw that they were bigger and riper than any of the other apples, and she at once began to plan how she could get them.

"I must consult Marley about this matter," said the Apple Woman to herself.

Marley was the Apple Woman's hen. She was not at all clever, but in some ways she was very sensible, and she always had a very kind heart.

When Marley heard what the Apple Woman had to tell, she turned her head from side to side, looking at the Apple Woman, first with one round yellow eye and then with the other.

"We must not leave the apples on the tree," she said, "or the birds will come and eat them. On the other hand, you cannot climb the tree for them, because you know that your joints are stiff with rheumatism. But my joints are not stiff, and I have, moreover, a strong pair of wings, which you have not, so I will fly up to the tip-top of the tree where the apples are, and I will shake the bough until they fall."

"What a clever idea! You are a wonderful hen, Marley," said the Old Apple Woman joyfully, and they both went out. The Apple Woman stood under the tree, holding her apron to catch the apples as they fell, and Marley flew up to the tip-top of the apple tree.

But the bough on which the apples grew was slender and weak, and, on the other hand, Marley was heavy and fat; so when Marley alighted on the branch it gave way under her so far and so suddenly that Marley, much alarmed, flew off into the air, cackling with fright, and flapped her way down to the grass at the Old Woman's feet. But the apples still hung, red and ripe, at the tip-top of the apple tree.

"You did not get the apples, Marley," said the Apple Woman, much disappointed.

Marley was too much upset to answer. She walked up and down on the grass, cackling from sheer nervousness.

"You did not get the apples," repeated the Apple Woman.

"Apples?" clucked Marley. "What are three apples compared to my life? I might as well have broken my neck."

"That would have been dreadful," said the Apple Woman soothingly.

"It would have been very dreadful," replied Marley, looking at the Old Apple Woman, first with one yellow eye and then with the other.

"But since you have not broken anything," said the Apple Woman, "cannot you think of some other plan for reaching those three apples at the tip-top of the tree?"

"I cannot think of any other plan," said Marley shortly.

Then suddenly the Apple Woman began to smile and nod her head.

"But I have myself thought of a plan," she said. "I remember that the Leprechaun left his long ladder here the other day, because he said he was too tired to carry it home, and he has not yet come to fetch it. I will lean the Leprechaun's ladder against the tree, and though my joints are stiff with rheumatism, I am sure I shall be able to climb as high as those three red apples."

But Marley was offended, because she thought the Apple Woman had not made enough fuss over her, so she answered in a cold indifferent way:

"Yes, yes! I dare say you will be able to climb as high as the apples. I am now going to rest for a little. I do not feel at all well."

And Marley went into the house and shut the door.

The Apple Woman found the Leprechaun's long ladder, and she leaned it against the apple tree, and began to climb up—very slowly, because of her rheumatism. When she reached the top she stepped right off the ladder onto a bough of the tree, and putting up her hand, she found that she could just reach the apples. She pulled them, one by one, and put them into her great pockets, and then she turned to step back on the ladder again, intending to climb down as she had climbed up.

But a dreadful thing had happened while the Apple Woman was standing on the bough of the apple tree, pulling the apples. For the Leprechaun had come to fetch his ladder, and carry it home; and when he came up to the Old Apple Woman's house, he saw his ladder leaning against the tree; but he did not see the Apple Woman, who was hidden among the leaves.

"Why, here is my ladder," he said to himself, "and why should I disturb the Apple Woman and her good hen Marley by knocking at the door and asking for it? I will simply take my ladder and carry it away."

So he took it up and carried it away, and the Leprechaun was just out of sight when the Apple Woman turned round and found that the ladder was gone. She could scarcely believe her eyes.

"Marley!" she screamed. "Help! Marley! Come quick!"

Marley came running out when she heard the Apple Woman calling, but when she saw what had happened she could do nothing but cry and beat her wings in despair.

"What shall I do?" cried the Apple Woman. "Here I am on the tip-top of this terrible apple tree, and if I try to get down I shall certainly fall! Must I sit here for always and always and always?"

But Marley could only cry louder and beat her wings harder.

Now just then Michael happened to be passing near, and when he heard such a noise coming from the Apple Woman's house, he ran up to see what it was all about.

"Why do you cry so, Marley?" he said. "And why do you beat your wings?"

"How can I help it?" replied Marley. "Do you not see that the Old Apple Woman is on the tip-top of the apple tree, and cannot get down? She climbed up by the Leprechaun's long ladder, and when she turned to climb down again, the ladder was gone."

Michael thought very hard for a few minutes. Then he said:

"The Old Woman who keeps the goats has also a

long ladder. It is rather too heavy for me to carry alone, but if Teig the dog and the Eldest Goat were to help to carry it, we could bring it here and lean it against the tree, and if the Apple Woman climbed up by one long ladder, she could climb down by another."

"Oh, Michael," cried Marley and the Apple Woman together, "go quickly and fetch the ladder."

So Michael went, and before long he and Teig the dog and the Eldest Goat had brought up the ladder, and they leaned it carefully against the tree and held it steady while the Apple Woman climbed down.

When the Apple Woman was once more standing safely on the grass, she and her hen Marley cried with joy. Then the Apple Woman took the three big red apples out of her pockets and she gave them to Michael, and Teig the dog, and the Eldest Goat, one apple to each, as a reward for their kindness in helping her.

So Michael and Teig the dog and the Eldest Goat were happy, too.

*By Anne Casserley*

# THE BOJABI TREE

## I. ROBIN RAT

IN THE LAND of All-the-Beasts there was a GREAT HUN-
GER. Some of the animals who were so HUNGRY were
Tabby Tiger
  Bruno Bear
    Katy Crocodile
      Robin Rat
        Pinky Pig
          Giddy Goat
            Tommy Tortoise
and many more—more than you could ever count in a
year.

They ran around the wood, here and there and everywhere, eating roots and twigs and any old scraps they
could find. But still they were HUNGRY.

One day they came to a Big Tree full of fruit. But

they could not eat it, for they did not know what it was.

They sat down in a circle round the tree, and said, "What can we do?"

When they had thought a while, they said, "Let us send Robin Rat up the river to Leo, our King, and ask him what the fruit is and whether we may eat it."

Robin Rat was young and spry. He scuttled up the tree and brought down one of its fruit to show King Leo.

It was a DELICIOUS-looking fruit!

It looked like an

APPLEORANGEPEARPLUMBANANA

but it smelled like a

BANANAPLUMPEARORANGEAPPLE.

Then Robin Rat scuttled down to the river bank and climbed into his little canoe.

All the day and all the day he paddled

and paddled

and PADDLED

up the river.

And the Great Red Sun dropped behind the trees.

Then he found King Leo on the bank, all ready to receive visitors. He was wearing his crown tipped on the back of his head because he felt happy. He smiled at Robin Rat as pleasant as you please, and asked him to stay to supper.

After supper they curled up and went to sleep. There was nothing else to do, you see.

In the morning King Leo said politely, "What can I do for you, my small friend?"

Then Robin Rat answered, "Please tell us, King Leo,

what is the name of this tree and whether we may eat the fruit of it. We are all SO HUNGRY!"

King Leo looked at the fruit that was like an

APPLEORANGEPEARPLUMBANANA

and he sniffed at the fruit that was like a

BANANAPLUMPEARORANGEAPPLE.

Then he said, "It is a good fruit. You may eat it. The name of the tree is

BOJABI."

Then Robin Rat hung his cap over his right ear and climbed into his little canoe.

All the day and all the day he paddled down the great river.

And all the way he was thinking how much he could eat of that

DELICIOUS fruit.

And at night he came home.

All the Beasts were waiting for him on the shore. He came up, whisking his paddle *this* way and *that* way through the water, just to show how well he could do it.

"What is it, Robin Rat?" said All the Beasts. "Tell us the name!" they roared and howled and grunted and whined and shrieked and squealed, each in his own PARTICULAR voice.

"Oh!" said Robin Rat. "I knew it a while ago, but now I have clean forgotten."

Then All the Beasts stepped into the water and upset Robin Rat's little canoe.

They SPLASHED and they

SPLUTTERED and they

SP-L-ANKED

Robin Rat.

Squeaksqueaksqueaksqueaksqueak!

Nobody heard a word more from *him* that day.


## II.  PINKY PIG

But now All the Beasts were HUNGRIER STILL.

They sat in a circle round the tree and thought a while.

Then they said, "Let us send Pinky Pig to King Leo to ask the name of the tree. But, Pinky Pig,

"DO NOT FORGET IT!"

Pinky Pig trotted away home—

trip-trap, trip-trap, trip-trap.

He put on his best blue coat and buttoned it up, though it squeezed him a little.

Then he trotted—trip-trap, trip-trap, trip-trap— down to his little rowboat and took his oars to row up the big river.

All the day and all the day he rowed
and he rowed
and he ROWED
up the big river.

And the Great Red Sun dropped behind the trees.

Then he found King Leo on the bank, all ready to receive visitors. His crown was a little crooked because he had put it on in a hurry when he saw Pinky Pig coming.

He smiled politely but he did not invite Pinky Pig to stay to supper.

"What can I do for you, my plump friend?" he asked.

Pinky Pig showed him the fruit that looked like an

APPLEORANGEPEARPLUMBANANA

and smelled like a

BANANAPLUMPEARORANGEAPPLE,

and said, "Please, King Leo, we must know the name of this tree or we cannot eat the fruit. Please be so kind as to tell us."

Then King Leo said,

"I have told Robin Rat.

"I will tell you.

"The name of the tree is

BOJABI!

"Do not forget it."

Pinky Pig trotted back to his rowboat—trip-trap, trip-trap, trip-trap.

All the night and all the night he rowed—he rowed —and he ro-o-owed until the oars—dropped—from— his—hands—and the big river took the boat down itself.

Pinky Pig curled up under the seat. And this is the sound that came from the boat:

H-r-r-r-umph

h-h-r-r-r-*umph*

h-h-h-r-r-r-r-UM-MPH!

In the morning Pinky Pig sat up and rubbed his eyes. He was at home. All the Beasts stood on the river bank looking at him. "What is it, Pinky Pig? Tell us the name!" they whistled and snarled and squealed and shrieked and whined and grunted and howled and roared, each in his own PARTICULAR voice.

"I know it," said Pinky Pig. Then he yawned.

"I knew it last night," he said, "but—ah—ah—I— must—have—been—asleep, and—ah—for—got—ten— it."

That is the way he talked when he was yawning.

Then All the Beasts jumped into the water and smashed Pinky Pig's boat and his oars.

They PLUNGED about and
    PUNCHED poor Pinky Pig and
    POUNDED him until he went
plop—plop—into the water.

SQue-e-e-e-e-e-E-E-E-E-E-E-E-AL!

He ran home with the water running off him and making little puddles here and there.

Nobody heard a word more from *him* that day.

### III. GIDDY GOAT

But now All the Beasts were HUNGRIER and HUNGRIER. They could have eaten nails if there had been any nails in the Great Wood.

They sat in a circle round the tree and thought a while.

Then they said, "Giddy Goat is older than Pinky Pig, and wiser than Robin Rat. Let us send him to King Leo to ask the name of the tree, so that we may eat the fruit of it before we starve. But, Giddy Goat,

"Do NOT FORGET IT!"

"A-rashum!" said Giddy Goat. He was afraid of catching cold. Away he ran—ker-lipp, ker-lipp—to his house to get a big woolly muffler to wear on the river. He wrapped it three times round his neck and tucked it neatly under his beard.

Then he ran—ker-lipp, ker-lipp—down to his little sailboat on the river.

All the day and all the day he sailed
> and he sailed
> and he SAILED

up the big river.

And the Great Red Sun dropped behind the trees.

Then he found King Leo on the bank, *not* ready to receive visitors. His crown was on straight and he looked very CROSS.

"Whatdoyouwant?" he snapped—just like that.

"A-rashum!" said Giddy Goat. "I beg your Majesty's pardon. I have a cold coming on."

He showed King Leo the fruit that looked like an

> APPLEORANGEPEARPLUMBANANA

and smelled like a

> BANANAPLUMPEARORANGEAPPLE,

and said, "If you would be so very kind, King Leo, to tell us the name of this tree, so that we may know whether we may eat the fruit of it . . ."

Then King Leo said,

"I have told Robin Rat.

"I have told Pinky Pig.

"I will tell you.

"But I will not tell ANYBODY ELSE.

"The name is

> BOJABI.

"DO NOT FORGET IT!"

"A-rash-oo!" said Giddy Goat, and he skipped away —ker-lipp, ker-lipp—to his sailboat.

All the night and all the night he sailed
> and he sailed
> and he SAILED.

All the way he was remembering the name, and he remembered it very well.

He sailed so fast that he got home in the early, early morning.

And all the way, when he wasn't remembering the name, he was sneezing:

"A-tchoo! A-rashum! A-tchoo!"

All the beasts were waiting for him—rows and rows of them. Those in the back rows looked over the shoulders of those in the front rows, or climbed on their backs.

They pushed and jostled one another until they had upset Giddy Goat's sailboat. Ker-splash!—he went into the river.

Such a sight as he was when they pulled him out! His long hair was full of water. His beard was full of water. His eyes were full of water. His beautiful new muffler was full of water.

When the animals crowded round him to ask the name of the tree, he shook himself so that the water flew in their faces, and ran away home—ker-lipp, ker-lipp—with a most dreadful

A-TCHOO!

His wife made him go to bed. And not one word could anyone get from him all that day but "A-tchoo! A-rashum! A-TCHOO!"


IV.  TOMMY TORTOISE

By this time All the Beasts were so HUNGRY that they sat round the tree and cried.

You see, there was no one else who had a boat.

"What shall we do?" they wailed and howled and buzzed and grunted and groaned and sobbed and lamented, each in his own most PARTICULAR voice.

Then Tommy Tortoise, who had been lying asleep in the sun, opened one eye, and said, "What is all this fuss about? Haven't you found out the name of this tree YET?"

They said they had not and cried harder than ever.

"Oh, well," said he, "if that's all, I'll go and get it for you."

"YOU!" snarled Tabby Tiger.

"You! You!" grunted Bruno Bear.

"You!" snapped Katy Crocodile, biting her word off short.

"You-u-u-u!" trumpeted Elizabeth Elephant.

"You! You! You!" chattered Mimi Monkey.

You never heard such a noise—not even at the circus —as there was when they all said this, each in his own PARTICULAR voice.

"Yes, me—I mean *I,*" said Tommy Tortoise in his little, thin voice.

Then he crawled slowly home, trailing one foot after the other, as some boys do on their way to school.

He found his mother knitting stockings and rocking the baby.

"Hssh!" said Mrs. Tortoise. "He's just dropping off."

"Mother," said Tommy Tortoise. "How can I remember the name of that tree if I go up the river to get it?"

"Tommy," said Mrs. Tortoise, "do you remember

how you used to go to school with all the other little tortoises and learn things?"

"Yes," said Tommy.

> "Nine times one makes nine,
>
> "Nine times two makes eighteen,
>
> "Nine times three makes twenty-seven—"

He said the Nines table because anybody can say the Tens, and he wasn't sure about the Elevens.

"Hsh!" said Mrs. Tortoise. "That will do. You will wake the baby.

"But I will tell you how to remember." She whispered in his ear.

Then she said, "Now, Tommy, whatever happens to you, mind your manners. Remember to bow to King Leo and to speak to him so politely that he will know you have been well brought up."

"Yes, Mother," said Tommy Tortoise.

Then he put on his cap with the red tassel, and he went down to the river. He had no boat; so he had to swim.

> All the day and all the day he swam
>
> and he swam
>
> and he SWAM.

When he was tired swimming, he would turn over on his shell and float with all his legs kicking in the water, just as the baby kicks in his bath.

And the Great Red Sun dropped behind the trees.

When Tommy Tortoise reached King Leo's home, King Leo was NOT curled up comfortably wearing his crown and ready to receive visitors. He was standing on the river bank waving his tail. His big head was wag-

gling *this* way and *that* way, and he was not smiling
AT ALL.

Before Tommy could speak a word, or even make his
best bow, King Leo said:

"R-R-R-R-R-R-R-R-R-R-R-R-R-R-R-R! S-s-cat! S-scamper!
S-scat! S-skedaddle!

"I told Robin Rat.

"I told Pinky Pig.

"I told Giddy Goat.

"I WILL NOT TELL YOU
that the name of the tree is bojabi.

"R-R-R-R-R-R-R-R-R-R-R-R-R-R-R-R-R!"

"Bojabi," whispers Tommy Tortoise to himself, and
jumps—ker-lump—into the river again.

All the night and all the night he swam
and he swam
and he SWAM.
But it was easy work to let the big river carry him on its
back.

All the night and all the night he made up a little
song and sang it, like this:

"O Robin Rat, what shall we eat?
Bojabi—bojabi—bojabi.
O Pinky Pig, so fat and neat,
Bojabi—bojabi—bojabi.
O Giddy Goat, so fast and fleet,
Bojabi—bojabi—bojabi.
O Humpy Hippo, hard to beat,
Bojabi—bojabi—bojabi.
O Bruno Bear, with clumsy feet,

Bojabi—bojabi—bojabi.
O Katy Crocodile, here's a treat,
Bojabi—bojabi—bojabi.
O Tommy Tortoise, of Puddle Street,
Bojabi—bojabi—bojabi.
O All the Beasts, come quick and eat
Bojabi—bojabi—bojabi."

And THAT was what his mother had told him to do.

All the Beasts were lying on the bank of the river. Far away they heard the little, thin voice of Tommy Tortoise singing his song. They pricked up their ears, looking *this* way and *that* way as they listened.

And presently Tommy Tortoise came crawling up through the mud.

"What is it?" they cried, each in his own PARTICULAR voice. You would have thought that all the circuses in the world were there.

"Bojabi," said Tommy Tortoise, and crawled away home without another word.

That night All the Beasts had bojabi for their supper.

But Tommy Tortoise had cream with his.

After that All the Beasts in that wood were never hungry. They could always eat bojabi.

They made Tommy Tortoise their king. "For," they said, "if he could remember the name of the bojabi tree, he can do anything."

As far as I know he is king of All the Beasts in the Great Wood today.

—Adapted from an African Folk Tale.

*By Edith Rickert*

## LIVING IN W'ALES

ONCE THERE WAS a man who said he didn't like the sort of houses people lived in, so he built a model village. It was not really like a model village at all, because the houses were all big enough for real people to live in, and he went about telling people to come and live in W'ales.

There was also living in Liverpool a little girl who was very nice. So when all the people went off with the man to live in W'ales, she went with them. But the man walked so fast that presently some of them got left behind. The ones who were left behind were the little girl, and an Alsatian dog, and a very cross old lady in a bonnet and black beads, who was all stiff, but had a nice husband, who was left behind too.

So they went along till they came to the sea; and in the sea was a whale. The little girl said, "That was what he meant, I suppose, when he talked about living in W'ales. I expect the others are inside: or, if not, they are in another one. We had better get in this one."

So they shouted to know if they might come in, but the whale didn't hear them. The nice husband said that if that was what living in W'ales meant, he would rather go back to Liverpool; but the horrid old lady said, "Nonsense! I will go and whisper in its ear."

But she was very silly, and so instead of whispering in its ear she went and tried to whisper in its blowhole. Still the whale didn't hear; so she got very cross and said, "None of this nonsense, now! Let us in at once! I won't have it, do you hear? I simply won't stand it!" and she began to stir in his blowhole with her umbrella.

So the whale blew, like an enormous sneeze, and blew her right away up into the sky on top of the water he blew out of his hole, and she was never seen again. So then the nice husband went quietly back to Liverpool.

But the little girl went to the whale's real ear, which was very small and not a bit like his blowhole, and whispered into it, "Please, nice whale, we would so like to come in, if we may, and live inside." Then the whale opened his mouth, and the little girl and the Alsatian dog went in.

When they got right down inside, of course, there was no furniture. "He was quite right," said the little girl. "It is certainly not a bit like living in a house."

The only thing in there was a giant's wig that the whale had once eaten. So the little girl said, "This will do for a doormat." So she made it into a doormat, and the Alsatian dog went to sleep on it.

When he woke up again he started to dig holes; and, of course, it gave the whale most terrible pains to have holes dug by such a big dog in his inside, so he went up to the top of the water and shouted to the Captain of a ship to give him a pill. On board the ship there was a cold dressed leg of mutton that the Captain was tired of, so he thought, "That will make a splendid pill to give the whale." So he threw it to the whale, and the whale swallowed it; and when it came tobogganing down the whale's throat the Alsatian dog, who was very hungry, ate it, and stopped digging holes; and when the dog stopped digging holes the whale's pain went away. So he said "Thank you" to the Captain. "That was an excellent pill."

The Captain was very surprised that his pill had made the whale well again so soon; he had really done it only to get rid of the cold mutton.

But the poor little girl wasn't so lucky as the Alsatian dog. *He* had a doormat to sleep on, and something to eat. But there was no bed, and the little girl couldn't possibly sleep without a bed to sleep on; and she had nothing to eat—and this went on for days and days.

Meanwhile the whale began to get rather worried about them. He had swallowed them without thinking much about it; but he soon began to wonder what was happening to them, and whether they were comfortable. He knew nothing at all about little girls. He thought she would probably want something to eat by now, but he didn't know at all what. So he tried to talk down into his own inside, to ask her. But that is very difficult; at any rate, *he* couldn't do it. The words all came out instead of going in.

So he swam off to the tropics, where he knew a parrot, and asked him what to do. The parrot said it was quite simple, and flew off to an island where there was a big snake. He bit off its head and bit off its tail, and then flew back to the whale with the rest of it. He put most of the snake down the whale's throat, so that one end just came up out of its mouth.

"There," he said, "now you have a speaking tube. You speak into one end of the snake, and the words will go down it inside you."

So the whale said "Hello" into one end of the snake, and the little girl heard "Hello" come out of the other. "What do you want?" said the whale. "I want something to eat," said the little girl. The whale told the parrot, "She wants something to eat. What do little girls eat?"

"Little girls eat rice pudding," said the parrot. He had one, in a big glass bowl; so he poured it down the snake too, and it came down the other end and the little girl ate it.

When she had eaten it she caught hold of her end of the snake, and called "Hello!" up it.

"Hello!" said the whale.

"May I have a bed?" said the little girl.

"She wants a bed," the whale said to the parrot.

"You go to Harrod's for that," said the parrot, "which is the biggest shop in London," and flew away.

When the whale got to Harrod's, he went inside. One of the shopwalkers came up to him and said, "What can I do for *you,* please?" which sounded very silly.

"I want a bed," said the whale.

"Mr. Binks, BEDS!" The shopwalker called out very loud, and then ran away. He was terribly frightened, because there had never been a whale in the shop before.

Mr. Binks the Bed Man came up and looked rather worried.

"I don't know that we have got a bed that will exactly fit you, sir," he said.

"Why not, silly?" said the whale. "I only want an ordinary one."

"Yes, sir," said the Bed Man, "but it will have to be rather a large ordinary one, won't it?"

"Of course not, silly," said the whale. "On the contrary, it will have to be rather a small one."

He saw a very nice little one standing in a corner.

"I think that one will just about fit me," he said.

"You can have it if you like," said the Bed Man. "But I think it's you who are the silly to think a little bed like that will fit you!"

"I want it to fit me *inside,* of course," said the whale, "not *outside!* . . . Push!" and he opened his mouth.

So they all came and pushed, and sure enough it just did fit him. Then he ate all the pillows and blankets he could find, which was far more than was needed really, and when it all got down inside, the little girl made the bed and went to sleep on it.

So the whale went back to the sea. Now that the little

girl and the Alsatian dog both had had something to eat and somewhere to sleep, they said:

"The man was right, it really is much more fun living in W'ales than living in houses."

So they stayed on.


P.S. The parrot went on feeding them, not always on rice pudding.

*By Richard Hughes*

## THE SADDLER'S HORSE

I WONDER how many of you who read this story have ever seen a cigar-store Indian?

I don't mean in pictures, or in someone's collection of old-fashioned curiosities, but a real one, all carved and painted and standing just where he should stand, on the sidewalk outside the cigar-store door. Not so many years ago a cigar-store Indian used to be quite an every-day sight, almost as common as a barber's pole. And as for saddler's horses, many a town that really was a town used to have one, and very proud they were of him.

I don't know where all the cigar-store Indians have

119

gone to. Perhaps they are living somewhere, here and there, in private families. Perhaps they have all migrated in a body to the great open spaces, or wherever it is that Wooden Indians do go. Certainly one does not see them any more on the sidewalk, kindly offering one a cigar or a pinch of snuff, as they used to do.

But I do know of one place where there is still a Saddler's Horse.

He is very big and tall, painted all over a pleasant varnishy dapple gray, and he stands outside what is still the saddler's store—though it sells other things as well nowadays—in the open space near the railroad station, just two minutes' walk from Mr. Murdle's store. All day long he stands there and dreams.

He dreams of the old days when there were no airplanes and no gas pumps; when the railroad station was very much smaller and the big hotel had not yet been built, nor the concrete highway; when it took country folk a whole day, instead of an hour, to get to town and back, and they drove in spring-top buggies and buckboards and farm wagons, and instead of parked cars by the sidewalk edge there were horses, long rows of them, tied in the shade to hitching posts under the big elm trees.

In those days the feed store and the hardware store and the saddler's were quite the most important stores in town. And the Saddler's Horse, standing out there with the very newest style of shiny harness buckled on his back for every passer-by to admire, would gaze down his nose at the country horses switching their tails under the elms, and feel that he was very, very superior.

But times have changed. There are gas pumps now instead of hitching posts. Automobiles and trucks go up and down the street; very few teams pass by, and the Saddler's Horse rarely sees a buggy at all. But still he stands there, all day long, watching the traffic go past, and at six o'clock, when the train whistle blows, the saddler wheels him indoors and puts him to bed for the night.

Just across the street is an antique shop. It happened that one day, not very long ago, the storekeeper came across a Wooden Indian. I don't know where he found him, but he brought him home, together with a grandfather clock and an old bureau and a print of a little girl hugging a kitten, and he stood him out on the sidewalk just beside the shop door.

As soon as the Wooden Indian saw the Saddler's Horse, and as soon as the Saddler's Horse caught sight of the Wooden Indian, they began to shout to each other across the street. The Saddler's Horse was very pleased. He hadn't seen a Wooden Indian for years and years. It was just like old times come back again.

"Hello," said the Indian. "What are you doing there? I haven't seen a horse like you for ages!"

"Oh, I live here," said the Saddler's Horse. "I'm the oldest person in this town! I've been here longer than the Town Hall itself."

"Well, well," said the Wooden Indian. "Times have surely changed, haven't they? None of these nasty automobiles when *we* were young! I don't like them, and I don't like the gas pumps, either. Things used to be much better. You and I are losing our jobs now. I've lost mine already. Antiques, that's what they call us nowadays! Still, I've spent the last five years in a barn, and it feels good to stand out on the sidewalk again and see the folks passing. I've always been used to an outdoor life, and I like it.  But tomorrow I suppose someone will come along and buy me, and then there'll be an end of it all—"

Just then a big truck passed by. It made so much noise that neither of them could hear the other speaking.

*"That's* what I complain of!" said the Saddler's Horse, when it had passed. "All that noise, and it shakes one to pieces! Yes, the old times were much better."

"Tell you what," cried the Wooden Indian as soon as he could make himself heard once more. "Suppose you and I take a trip together? We might never get the chance again! Everyone should have a good gallop once in his life. They think we are back numbers, here, but we'll show them! Come along!"

He hopped across the street, right between the automobiles, and made one spring to the back of the Saddler's Horse. The Saddler's Horse had no time even to think; he just threw up his head and snorted, and off they went! Out ran the antique dealer, out ran the saddler, waving his arms and shouting, but it was too late. The Saddler's Horse and the Wooden Indian were off together, and nothing could stop them!

First they galloped by the railroad station, dodging in and out among the jitneys and busses and parked cars; then up the hill, round the corner by the Post Office and into Main Street. Everyone turned and stared. Little boys yelled, shopkeepers ran to their door-

ways, old ladies dropped their parcels and screamed.
People shouted:

"It's a circus parade!"

"It's a new advertisement!"

"It's a wild Indian gone crazy!"

And among all the shouting and excitement the saddler and the antique dealer ran puffing and panting
along, shouting: "Stop them! Stop them!"

But no one could stop them.

Down Main Street they galloped, right through all
the traffic. The policeman ran out and blew his whistle
at them, but they dashed straight by him. Past the
cinema, past the bank and Town Hall, and when they
came to the tall Stop and Go sign on the corner the
Saddler's Horse jumped clear over it. Then his great
hoofs thundered over the bridge, and they were gone.

The townsfolk were left staring.

"Did you ever hear of such a thing!" they gasped.
The old gentlemen mopped their foreheads, and the old
ladies picked up their parcels again. "The idea of tearing along like that!" they cried indignantly. "Something ought to be done about it!" And as for the traffic
cop, he was as red in the face as a beetroot, and he
shouted and waved at the automobiles as if it were all
their fault.

The little boys craned their necks down the street.
They were still hoping to see the rest of the circus
parade.

Before long the news had gone out over the whole
countryside. Startled motorists pulled up at wayside gas

stations, telling of great hoofs that had thundered behind them along the highway, of a huge gray horse that had flashed by in a cloud of dust and disappeared. Up and down the state roads, far and wide, motor-cycle cops went whizzing past, looking everywhere for a crazy Indian on a big gray horse.

Meantime, many miles away in a green meadow by the roadside, the Wooden Indian and the Saddler's Horse had stopped to rest.

"That was a grand ride!" said the Wooden Indian as he slid off.

"It was!" panted the Saddler's Horse.

"Didn't we give them a scare?" said the Wooden Indian.

"We did!" puffed the Saddler's Horse.

To tell the truth, he was beginning to feel a bit tired, and was quite glad to stop galloping for a while and just rest quietly in the deep grass. It had been grand while it lasted, but now, all at once, his wooden limbs began to tremble and his wooden back began to ache. Tomorrow, he knew, he would be terribly stiff in all his joints. After all, when one is as old as the Saddler's Horse, and has never galloped before in one's life, one is bound to feel it!

Just then, somewhere in the distance, a train whistle blew; a long, plaintive note. The Saddler's Horse gave a start. He thought all at once of the sidewalk and the trees and the railroad station, the familiar street that he had gazed on for so many years. Six o'clock . . . at this very moment, perhaps, the saddler was stepping out of the doorway in his apron, ready to wheel him back into the cool, dark store to sleep for the night.

"Don't you think," said the Saddler's Horse in a rather shaky voice, "that we ought to be turning back now?"

"Back?" said the Wooden Indian. "I'm not going back! You can go if you want to, I shall stay here for the rest of my life and live in the woods!"

The Saddler's Horse looked doubtfully at the meadows, at the tall dark woods behind, and the sky already deepening to sunset.

"Well . . . good-by!" he said at last.

"Good-by!" said the Wooden Indian.

Slowly and stiffly the Saddler's Horse began to limp back along the dusty highroad toward town. Every once in a while he turned his head to gaze back. There in the middle of the field, grown each moment smaller and smaller, he could see the Wooden Indian standing, waving his arms, clear and distinct against the sunset.

The saddler felt not at all cheerful that evening as he stood in his doorway, staring across the street. For one thing, he was afraid that at any moment the policeman might come and arrest him, because of all the disturbance that had occurred. He had talked it over with the antique dealer and they had both decided that the wisest thing was to say nothing about it. Still, one never knew.

Besides, he really did miss the Horse. He was proud of him, and they had lived together so long that he was like an old friend. All these years the saddler had wheeled him out every morning, and wheeled him in to bed every night, and now goodness alone knew where he was or what had happened to him!

When the six o'clock whistle blew, the saddler had all he could do to keep from bursting into tears.

But next morning, when he opened the store door, his heart gave a great jump.

"Bless me!" cried the saddler.

For there in his old place on the sidewalk stood the Saddler's Horse, gazing down his nose at the automobiles just as usual. He looked a little dusty and perhaps a bit shaky on his legs, and of all strange things there was a burdock caught in his long tail! But otherwise he was none the worse. There he stood and there he stands to this day, perfectly contented, for he has never tried to run away again. You may see him yourself, any time between eight and six, if you happen to be passing by.

And as for the Wooden Indian, no one has ever set eyes on him again.

*By Margery Williams Bianco*

# HOW TO TELL CORN FAIRIES
## IF YOU SEE 'EM

IF YOU HAVE ever watched the little corn begin to
march across the black lands and then slowly change

127

to big corn and go marching on from the little corn moon of summer to the big corn harvest moon of autumn, then you must have guessed who it is that helps the corn come along. It is the corn fairies. Leave out the corn fairies and there wouldn't be any corn.

All children know this. All boys and girls know that corn is no good unless there are corn fairies.

Have you ever stood in Illinois or Iowa and watched the late summer wind or the early fall wind running across a big cornfield? It looks as if a big, long blanket were being spread out for dancers to come and dance on. If you look close and if you listen close you can see the corn fairies come dancing and singing—sometimes. If it is a wild day and a hot sun is pouring down while a cool north wind blows—and this happens sometimes— then you will be sure to see thousands of corn fairies marching and countermarching in mocking grand marches over the big, long blanket of green and silver. Then, too, they sing, only you must listen with your littlest and newest ears if you wish to hear their singing. They sing soft songs that go pla-sizzy pla-sizzy-sizzy, and each song is softer than an eye-wink, softer than a Nebraska baby's thumb.

And Spink, who is a little girl living in the same house with the man writing this story, and Skabootch, who is another little girl in the same house—both Spink and Skabootch are asking the question, "How can we tell corn fairies if we see 'em? If we meet a corn fairy how will we know it?" And this is the explanation the man gave to Spink who is older than Skabootch, and to Skabootch who is younger than Spink:

All corn fairies wear overalls. They work hard, the corn fairies, and they are proud. The reason they are proud is because they work so hard. And the reason they work so hard is because they have overalls.

But understand this. The overalls are corn gold cloth, woven from leaves of ripe corn mixed with ripe October corn silk. In the first week of the harvest moon coming up red and changing to yellow and silver the corn fairies sit by thousands between the corn rows weaving and stitching the clothes they have to wear next winter, next spring, next summer.

They sit cross-legged when they sew. And it is a law among them that each one must point the big toe at the moon while sewing the harvest moon clothes. When the moon comes up red as blood early in the evening they point their big toes slanting toward the east. Then toward midnight when the moon is yellow and halfway up the sky their big toes are only half slanted as they sit cross-legged sewing. And after midnight when the moon sails its silver disk high overhead and toward the west, then the corn fairies sit sewing with their big toes pointed nearly straight up.

If it is a cool night and looks like frost, then the laughter of the corn fairies is something worth hearing. All the time they sit sewing their next year clothes they are laughing. It is not a law they have to laugh. They laugh because they are half-tickled and glad because it is a good corn year.

And whenever the corn fairies laugh then the laugh comes out of the mouth like a thin gold frost. If you should be lucky enough to see a thousand corn fairies sitting between the corn rows and all of them laughing, you would laugh with wonder yourself to see the gold frost coming from their mouths while they laugh.

Travelers who have traveled far, and seen many things, say that if you know the corn fairies with a real knowledge you can always tell by the stitches in their clothes what state they are from.

In Illinois the corn fairies stitch fifteen stitches of ripe corn silk across the woven corn leaf cloth. In Iowa they stitch sixteen stitches, in Nebraska seventeen, and the farther west you go the more corn silk stitches the corn fairies have in the corn cloth clothes they wear.

In Minnesota one year there were fairies with a blue sash of corn-flowers across the breast. In the Dakotas the same year all the fairies wore pumpkin-flower neckties, yellow four-in-hands and yellow ascots. And in one strange year it happened in both the states of Ohio and Texas the corn fairies wore little wristlets of white morning glories.

The traveler who heard about this asked many questions and found out the reason why that year the corn fairies wore little wristlets of white morning glories. He said, "Whenever fairies are sad they wear white. And this year, which was long ago, was the year men were tearing down all the old zigzag rail fences. Now those old zigzag rail fences were beautiful for the fairies because a hundred fairies could sit on one rail and thousands and thousands of them could sit on the zigzags and sing pla-sizzy pla-sizzy, softer than an eye-wink, softer than a baby's thumb, all on a moonlit summer night. And they found out that year was going

to be the last year of the zigzag rail fences. It made
them sorry and sad, and when they are sorry and sad
they wear white. So they picked the wonderful white
morning glories running along the zigzag rail fences
and made them into little wristlets and wore those
wristlets the next year to show they were sorry and sad."

Of course, all this helps you to know how the corn
fairies look in the evening, the night time and the
moonlight. Now we shall see how they look in the day
time.

In the day time the corn fairies have their overalls
of corn gold cloth on. And they walk among the corn
rows and climb the corn stalks and fix things in the
leaves and stalks and ears of the corn. They help it to
grow.

Each one carries on the left shoulder a mouse brush
to brush away the field mice. And over the right shoulder each one has a cricket broom to sweep away the
crickets. The brush is a whisk brush to brush away mice
that get foolish. And the broom is to sweep away
crickets that get foolish.

Around the middle of each corn fairy is a yellow
belly belt. And stuck in this belt is a purple moon shaft
hammer. Whenever the wind blows strong and nearly
blows the corn down, then the fairies run out and take
their purple moon shaft hammers out of their yellow
belly belts and nail down nails to keep the corn from
blowing down. When a rain storm is blowing up terrible and driving all kinds of terribles across the cornfield, then you can be sure of one thing. Running like
the wind among the corn rows are the fairies, jerking

their purple moon shaft hammers out of their belts and nailing nails down to keep the corn standing up so it will grow and be ripe and beautiful when the harvest moon comes again in the fall.

Spink and Skabootch ask where the corn fairies get the nails. The answer to Spink and Skabootch is, "Next week you will learn all about where the corn fairies get the nails to nail down the corn if you will keep your faces washed and your ears washed till next week."

And the next time you stand watching a big cornfield in late summer or early fall, when the wind is running across the green and silver, listen with your littlest and newest ears. Maybe you will hear the corn fairies going pla-sizzy pla-sizzy-sizzy, softer than an eye-wink, softer than a Nebraska baby's thumb.

*By Carl Sandburg*

## THE LOST MERBABY

ONCE UPON A TIME there were a fisherman and his wife who lived in a little stone house by the sea. It was only a tiny house, but that was no matter, for it was so neat and pretty that no one could wish it to be different. There was a creeper climbing on the wall, and a pot of flowers in each little window; and in the little kitchen there was a tall old clock, and a dresser with rows of blue platters, and there were two chairs and a round table and a carved oak settle, and by the fireside was a wooden cradle.

But the cradle was empty.

"A baby would be so troublesome," said the fisherman's wife. "How should I keep my little house neat and clean with a baby to mind?"

"A baby may be very well in its way," said the fisherman, "but we are happier as we are."

Every day the fisherman set the sails of his boat and went out to sea, and every day his wife went busily about and about the little house. And when her work was done she took her knitting and sat beside the door. She would watch the clouds wandering across the sky, and the waves breaking on the sand, and the sea-gulls wheeling above the cliffs, and then at last she would see the little boat come sailing into the bay, and she would run down to the beach to wave a welcome to the fisherman as soon as he should be near enough to see it.

"Who could be happier than we?" said they.

Now not so very far away there was another little home, but it could not be seen from the fisherman's house however hard one looked, for it lay under the sea. It was only a sandy hollow among the rocks, but it was set about so prettily with sea-weeds that it could not be bettered; and in the hollow lived four little mermaids and a merbaby.

The little mermaids loved the merbaby dearly, but for all that they often found her a great deal of trouble.

"Oh dear!" they would sigh, "how glad we shall be when she is grown up! She is sure to want us if we swim far away; and see how she plays with our sea-weeds and spoils them, and how she disturbs the sand in our little hollow when we have taken care to make it smooth. She is the most beautiful merbaby that could be," said they, "but she is rather a nuisance sometimes."

Now it happened one day that they found a round basket, such as the fishermen use, floating on the waves.

"Here is a cradle for our baby!" cried they. "When we want to play we can lay her inside and the waves will rock her to sleep."

So they took the basket and stopped up the holes and

lined it with sea-weed, and then they put the baby inside. The baby laughed and crowed with delight, and the mermaids swam to their home in the hollow among the rocks. They tidied the sea-weed and smoothed the sand upon the floor, and when they swam back to the cradle and peeped inside the baby was fast asleep.

"See how useful a cradle can be!" they cried. "Now we can swim away to play, for she will not need us for a long, long time."

But the little mermaids had forgotten all about the wind and the tide, and while they were gone the basket was carried far away. It was carried so far that at last it came to the foot of the cliffs near the fisherman's house, and there it rolled over and the merbaby slipped into a rock pool among the anemones.

When the fisherman came sailing home he saw something shining at the foot of the cliffs, and as soon as he had brought his boat to land he went to find out what it could be. And it was the merbaby's hair shining like polished gold in the sun.

"Good lack!" cried the fisherman. "What have we here?"

The merbaby was very tired of being all alone and it held out its little arms and cried to be taken up.

What was there left for the fisherman to do but to lift the baby from the pool and hurry home with it as fast as he could?

The fisherman's wife was just as surprised as he. She took the baby in her arms and hushed it and sang to it and coaxed the smile back into its face.

"How it laughs and crows!" cried she. "Look! its

eyes are the color of the sea, and what a dear little tail it has! It is nearly as beautiful as a real baby."

Then they pulled out the wooden cradle and put the baby inside, and there it lay crooning happily to itself. The fisherman's wife kept running to look at it and sing to it, and the baby laughed to see her and tangled its tiny hands in her hair; and the fisherman brought it shells for toys and threaded them in a chain.

That was all well enough, but away under the sea things were not going well at all. The little mermaids had come back from their playing and were looking everywhere for the baby.

"Have you seen our baby?" they asked the plaice who were lying almost buried in the sand.

The largest plaice flicked the sand off itself, for it is not polite to speak to anyone with only your eyes showing. "I have not seen any merbabies for quite a long time," it said, "but that may be because I only see things that are above me on account of my eyes. Perhaps you have noticed my eyes are both on one side of my head," he said proudly; "we are not like other fishes."

"Our baby was in a cradle," explained the little mermaids. "It was only a round basket, but it rocked up and down on the waves and sent her to sleep as well as a real cradle could have done."

"Something that might have been your cradle floated overhead a little while ago," said the plaice. "That is the way it went. Now, if my eyes had been one on each side of my head I should never have seen it."

Away swam the little mermaids, but no sign of the merbaby could they find.

Presently they met a porpoise. "Have you seen our baby?" they asked, and told him all the tale.

"This is very sad business," said the porpoise. "Come with me and we will see what can be done."

So they swam away together and asked all the fishes they met for news of the merbaby. Not one of them had seen her, but they were so sorry for the little mermaids that they all joined in the search.

The fisherman stood at the door of his house. "There is no wind," said he. "But look how strangely the sea is tossing!"

How could he know the waves were made by the mermaids and fishes as they looked for the lost baby?

"Let us look for her in the rock pools under the cliffs," said the little mermaids.

The lobsters came out of their holes to see what was wanted.

"We have lost our baby," said the mermaids. "We used to think she was only a nuisance, but now she is lost we are sure we can never be happy until she is found." And they told them all about it.

The lobsters waved their legs in surprise. "How strange to mind losing a baby!" said they. "We never take any notice of our own."

The eldest lobster drew his claws thoughtfully among his feelers. "There is a nasty wicker thing over there that might be your baby's cradle," said he. "It looks too much like a lobster trap for my taste, but as you are not lobsters perhaps you will not mind going near it."

Away went the little mermaids, and among the rocks

they found the basket they had used for a cradle. But there was no baby in it.

A big crab came sidling toward them.

"You look as unhappy as though you had just cast your shells," he said. "What can be the matter?"

Then the mermaids told their sorrowful tale all over again and the crab was very sad for them. He went up and down the rock pools explaining what had happened to everything he met, to the fishes and the shrimps and the sea-horses and the whelks, but not one of them could tell him anything.

At last he came to the anemones. "Have you seen the merbaby?" he asked.

"How could we see it?" asked the anemones. "We have no eyes."

"How dreadful to have no eyes!" exclaimed the crab, popping his own in and out with horror at the thought.

"It is not dreadful at all," said the anemones. "We have dozens of feelers and they are much more sensible than eyes, we think."

"But I can't help being sorry for you," said the crab. "Why, even if the mermaids' baby was here you could not see her, and she is worth seeing, they say. Her hair is golden yellow and her eyes are the color of the sea."

"What does it matter what color hair may be as long as it is hair?" said the biggest anemone crossly. "There is a piece twisted around one of my feelers now and it is most uncomfortable."

The crab brought the mermaids to look. He twiddled his eyes in great excitement. "See what I have found!" cried he.

One of the mermaids gently untangled the hair, and it was so fine and so shining that it could have belonged to no one but a merbaby.

"Our baby has been here," said they, "but where can she be now?"

The puffins came waddling along to see what was the matter. They looked very wise indeed when they heard all there was to be told.

"Now we come to think of it . . ." began one.

"We don't think often, you know," said the others, "But when we do we think to some purpose."

"When we come to think of it," said the first puffin again, "we saw the fisherman pick a merbaby from that very pool where you were talking to the anemones."

"Oh, tell us what he did with her!" cried the little mermaids.

"He took it home, of course," said the puffins. "Your baby is not lost now because we have told you where she is."

And they waddled away.

"Alas!" cried the mermaids. "We are scarcely any better off than when we did not know where to find her. The fisherman's house lies far beyond the reach of the waves and we can only go where the waves can carry us."

Then the mermaids lifted themselves out of the water. "Sea-gulls! Sea-gulls!" they cried. "Fly to the fisherman's house and tell us what has become of our baby."

So the sea-gulls flew across the sand and round and round the fisherman's house.

"Surely there is a storm coming," said the fisherman, "else why should the gulls fly so near and cry so loudly?"

How could he know they had come to see what was done with the merbaby?

"The fisherman has put the baby in the cradle and his wife is tending it as though it was their own," said the sea-gulls when they came back. Then the little mermaids began to weep and sigh. "If they grow to love our baby they will never give her to us again," they sobbed.

"How the sea moans tonight!" said the fisherman. "There is surely a storm coming."

But when the merbaby heard it she began to wail and would not be comforted. "Hush, hush!" soothed the fisherman's wife and ran to pick the baby out of the cradle, but the baby only wailed the more pitifully.

"It is the moaning of the sea that distresses her," said the fisherman's wife. "I could almost weep myself for the sorrowful sound of it." And she shut her window.

How could she know the baby cried because she knew the sound was the mermaid's weeping?

Now, as was only to be expected, the news of the merbaby spread among the fisherfolk, and they one and all made some excuse to come tapping at the fisherman's door.

The fisherman's wife showed the baby proudly. "Look what beautiful eyes she has!" she would say. "And see her tiny hands and the shining of her hair!"

"Yes! yes!" said the fisherfolk, "but it is a great pity that she has a tail."

"It is a very beautiful tail," said the fisherman's wife.

"And there are so many people with feet that to have a
tail is to be quite distinguished."

"A tail will be very awkward when she grows up,"
said the fisherfolk shaking their heads. "Why don't you
put her back in the sea?"

"How cruel that would be!" cried the fisherman's
wife. "She is far too tiny to care for herself. Besides, we
love her too much to part with her now."

So the merbaby lay from day to day in the wooden
cradle and cooed and crooned to itself. The fisherman
would leave the mending of his nets to play with it, and
his wife sang it gay little songs as she went about her
work and ran to kiss its tiny hands and cover it with
caresses.

"How could we think a baby was too much trouble!"
cried they. "A baby is the loveliest thing in the world."

But the little mermaids in their home among the
rocks had no heart to tend the sea-weeds, nor to smooth
the sand upon the floor and make all neat and tidy; they
had no heart to talk to the fishes, nor to play as they had
done before.

"How could we think our baby a trouble?" cried
they.

"Perhaps some day the fisherman's wife may tire of
her," said the eldest.

So every day they swam to the foot of the cliffs. "Sea-
gulls! Sea-gulls!" they cried. "Fly away and bring news
of our baby!"

And every day the sea-gulls told how the fisherman's
wife was fondling the baby as though it were her own.

"Alas! Alas!" wept the little mermaids. "We shall never see our baby again."

And every day when the merbaby heard the sound of their crying it began to wail and would not be comforted.

Then the fisherman would shake his head and ponder. "'Tis strange," said he, "the moaning of the sea is as the sound of someone weeping."

His wife, too, would ponder on the strangeness as she tried to hush the baby's crying, and she pondered so long that in the end she could not help but find the truth.

"Hark!" cried she. "The baby weeps in answer to the sound. It is no moaning of the waves we hear, but the sorrowing of those who have lost her."

Then she lifted the baby from the cradle and kissed it on this cheek and that, and ran with it to the shore. There sat the little mermaids weeping, and when they saw the fisherman's wife they held out their arms.

"Give us our baby!" cried they. "We cannot play nor sing nor be happy till we have her again."

"Sorrow no more. Here is your baby," said the fisherman's wife, and she kissed it over and over and gave it to them.

But when she came back to the little house and saw the empty cradle she fell to weeping as sadly as ever the little mermaids had done.

"It is my turn to sorrow now," said she.

And the fisherman could find no words to comfort her, for he was as sad as she.

But the little mermaids were happier than they had ever been before, and they swam up and down with the baby to tell all the sea-creatures of their good fortune and to thank them for their help.

"You look much happier than you did," said the crabs," but, "It is rather hard to understand family life," said the puffins. "We think a great deal of our babies, but of course they are much nicer than mer-babies because they have down and feathers."

"And wings," added the sea-gulls. "We cannot imagine what use arms can be."

The anemones shut up as soon as the mermaids came near. "We are glad you have found the baby, since it pleases you so much," said they. "But do take her away or we shall get hair all over us again."

The fishes looked at the merbaby very curiously. "Her tail is very fine," they said, "but a fin or two would improve her."

"Or having both her eyes on one side of her head," said the plaice.

"But of course if you are satisfied with her there is nothing more to be said," added the porpoise, and waved his flipper as he swam away.

The little mermaids hugged and kissed their baby. "Fancy thinking she is not perfect!" they cried. "Only the fisherman and his wife know how to love her as we do, and now they are sorrowful because we have taken her back again."

So sometimes they swam to the little bay and called, and the fisherman's wife would hear them and come running to the edge of the sea. Then the mermaids would give her the baby, and she would sit on the rocks to play with it and fondle it.

"It is so lonely now that the cradle is empty," she would sigh for sympathy. "We will come again soon," said they.

But one day when they swam to the bay, though they called and called, the fisherman's wife did not come running out to greet them.

"What can have befallen her?" they asked one another.

Then they lifted themselves out of the water. "Sea-gulls! Sea-gulls!" they cried. "Fly away across the sand and tell us why the fisherman's wife does not hear us calling."

So the sea-gulls flew round and round the little house as they had done before.

"You need not sorrow longer for the loneliness of the fisherman's wife," said they. "There is another baby in the cradle; it has feet instead of a tail and its eyes are the color of the sky, but she does not seem to mind, nor does the fisherman. They have not heard you call because they are too happy to hear anything but their own joy."

Then the little mermaids swam back to the hollow among the rocks.

"Now we can be happy all day long," said they, "for there is no one left lonely and sorrowing. And some day we will go again to the bay and the fisherman's wife will show us her baby and we will love it next to our own."

*By Margaret Baker*

# THE SONG OF THE LITTLE DONKEY

COLUMBUS, a small gray donkey, was being made ready for a journey. He stood very still while his master put his bridle on him and hitched him to the shafts of the cart, but when at last his little bell was fastened to his bridle he shook his head, so that the bell sent forth a series of tinkling notes. Columbus liked this sound: it made him feel cheerful.

"Just a minute now and we'll be off," his master said to him. "But first I have to load the cart." Columbus moved his ears back and forth to show he understood, and then shut his eyes while he waited.

But though his eyes were shut, he knew just what was happening. His master was carrying chairs from the house and putting them onto the cart. They were fine, dark chairs, so beautifully polished that they looked like satin, and Columbus knew that when the word to start was given he must walk very carefully, so that these chairs would not joggle against each other and get marred and scratched.

Several times each year the little donkey and his master made a journey from the small house by the side of the road, to a great city not far away. The cart was always filled with chairs when they started and always empty when they returned, for Columbus' master was such a fine cabinet-maker that he never had any trouble at all in selling the things he made.

And chairs were the things he liked best to make. "They are so friendly," he told Columbus, "for they are always inviting us to sit down and rest. And they provide a seat at the table when mealtime comes. The world would be a dreary place without chairs."

The old cabinet-maker often talked like this to his donkey, because he lived alone and had no one else to talk to. And Columbus always listened politely. The cabinet-maker and his donkey were good friends and got along well together, but there was one thing about which they could *not* agree and that was—roads. Each time they started to the city, the old cabinet-maker wanted to go straight along and get there as soon as possible. But Columbus wanted to explore, and always tried to turn in at the lanes and byways, because he felt sure he would find something there that was new and interesting.

Whenever he did this his master would give the lines a jerk and say: "No, no, Columbus. We have no time now to discover new places. We must get to town so that I can sell my chairs." And Columbus would have to give up the lanes and byways and go straight along.

Today, when the cart was loaded, the old cabinet-maker climbed into the driver's seat and picked up the

lines as he always did. "Giddap!" he said, making a
little clucking noise, and Columbus opened his eyes,
shook a few tinkles from his bell and trotted off.

The old cabinet-maker turned his head for a last
look at his house. "It's a funny thing," he told his little
donkey, "the way I feel today. I love my home better
than any place on earth. I love the hills around it; I
love Butterfly Brook that runs just behind it; and I
love the trees and flowers that grow beside it. I don't
like cities and never did—they are too crowded. But
today I am glad to be going to the city. I am lonesome
for the sound of children's voices. I want to hear them
laugh and watch them play. Maybe it's because it's
spring that I feel like this. Maybe the spring has got
into my blood."

Columbus put his ears back and listened. There was
a glad note in his master's voice that he had never heard
before, and it made the little donkey so happy that he
opened his mouth and sang. At least he *meant* it for
singing, though really it was not so very musical.

"You understand how I feel, don't you, old fellow?"
laughed the cabinet-maker. "Well, I'll tell you something else. Today, after I sell my chairs, I am going to
find some place where children are playing, and we are
going to stop and watch them, you and I. We are going to watch them even though it makes us late in getting back to Butterfly Brook."

Columbus tried to pay attention to what his master
was saying, but his mind wandered. For just ahead he
saw a shady lane running off from the highway. It was
an inviting lane and the little donkey hastened his steps.

He would turn in there, he thought, and have a look at it. Surely on a day like this, when the air smelled so good and the grass was so green, his master would not mind stopping for a little while.

But when he turned toward the entrance to the lane his master gave the usual jerk on the lines. "Not today, Columbus," he said. "Someday when we have more time I'll let you explore all you want to; but not now." And so, once again, the little donkey had to go straight along.

"Here's the place we'll stop first," the old cabinet-maker said, when they had reached the city and traveled along one of its wide streets until they came to a hand-some house. Columbus stopped obediently and looked around him.

The house stood well back on a beautiful lawn, and was surrounded by great trees and beds of blooming flowers. It looked even more inviting than the shady lane, he thought, and he wished he could go in and nibble some grass. But around this lawn was a high iron fence and there seemed to be no way of getting through it.

"Stand still, Columbus," the cabinet-maker told him, "and I'll go and ring the bell, there by the gate. I hope there's someone at home."

Climbing down from the cart, he pushed the bell, and at once a tall servant hurried forward.

"Good morning," said the old cabinet-maker. "If your master is at home, I should like to show him some chairs."

The tall servant looked at the cabinet-maker, and

then at Columbus, and then at the cart. "My master is at home," he said, "but I don't believe you had better try to sell him anything today. He's not in a very good humor."

"Oh, that doesn't matter," the cabinet-maker answered. "He will be in a good humor when he sees my chairs."

The tall servant opened the gate. "Very well," he said. "You may drive your little donkey up to the house. You'll find my master on the front porch, but don't blame *me* if he's cross with you."

Columbus could scarcely believe it when the cabinet-maker took him by the bridle and led him through the gate. He was going into the beautiful yard after all, he thought, and at once he started for the flower beds.

"Keep your donkey off the grass!" shouted the tall servant. And he sounded so stern that Columbus knew it was no use; he would have to go straight along.

"Good morning," said Columbus' master to the man who was sitting on the porch. "I am the cabinet-maker of Butterfly Brook, and I should like to show you my chairs."

"I don't want to see them," growled the man on the porch. "I have no use for any more chairs, because I live alone."

"I live alone, too," the cabinet-maker told him, "but I like to have lots of chairs around me. Chairs are good friends."

"Hump!" growled the man again. "I don't care for friends."

"That's too bad," said the cabinet-maker, shaking his

head and looking off across the wide lawn to where a fountain sparkled in the sunshine. "I should think you'd want to have someone to enjoy all this beauty with you. This yard would be a fine place for children to play in."

"Children!" shouted the man, jumping to his feet. "They would trample my grass and pick my flowers and throw stones in my fountain! They're a nuisance, children are. Look there," he went on, pointing across the lawn to the side fence. "See those children? They come here every day and stare at me and my lawn, but I never let them in."

The old cabinet-maker looked at the children pressing their faces against the fence. "Dear, dear," he said sadly. "I don't see how you have the heart to keep them out. One reason I came to town today was to see children. I wanted to watch them play, and to hear them shout and laugh."

The cabinet-maker's voice was so sad that Columbus stopped admiring the soft green grass, and shook his little bell as hard as he could, to make things sound more cheerful. And when he did this, the children outside the yard broke into peals of laughter.

"Do it again, little donkey. Shake your bell again!" they cried.

Columbus not only shook his bell again for them, but he moved his ears back and forth and, after a moment, he lifted his head and sang as he had done that morning on the road.

At this, the children laughed so hard that their voices were like hundreds of silver bells all being rung at the same time.

The man on the porch leaned forward and listened to them. "Well, I declare," he said. "That sounds pretty, doesn't it?"

"Children's laughter is the prettiest sound in the world," the old cabinet-maker told him. "Why won't you let them come into your yard and play for a while? They won't hurt anything, and it will make them so happy that they will laugh a great deal. You'd like that, wouldn't you?"

"I believe I would," the man on the porch said slowly. "Somehow it sounds like spring, and makes me happier than I have been in years."

As he finished speaking he touched a bell on the table beside him. "Open the gates and invite the children in," he said when the tall servant appeared. "And then go and tell the cook to prepare a great deal of food —cookies and other things that children like. We'll have lunch out here on the lawn. And don't forget to fetch some food for the little donkey."

The old cabinet-maker tried to tell the man on the porch how fine he thought this was, but his words were drowned by the shouts and laughter of the children as they came trooping through the gate.

"Thank you for letting us in," they called. "We think you have the loveliest house and lawn in the world!"

"Do you?" said the man, smiling in spite of himself. "Well, make yourselves at home. There's a little stream at the back of the lawn that you might like to wade in."

"A stream! A stream!" cried the children, dashing away. "We're going to wade in a stream!"

When they had gone, the man on the porch turned to

the old cabinet-maker. "I have changed my mind about your chairs," he said. "I am going to buy all of them— for the children to sit on when they eat their lunch. Unload them from the cart, and turn your little donkey loose to graze on my lawn. He ought to have some pleasure, too."

Columbus could scarcely wait until his master unhitched him. And when this was done he walked off across the lawn, nibbling as he went. Nothing like this had ever happened to him before, and he was so happy that he kicked his heels to show how glad he was to be alive on this fine spring morning.

And a fine spring morning it was for everyone. The children played leap frog and tag and blind-man's buff, while the two men sat on the porch and watched them. They rode Columbus up and down the garden paths and, at last, they all sat down to such a luncheon as they had never eaten before.

When they had eaten all they could hold, they gathered round the master of the house to thank him and say good-by. "I'm glad you have had a good time," he told them. "But don't thank *me* for it. The thanks belong partly to the cabinet-maker of Butterfly Brook, and partly to the springtime. But mostly they belong to the little donkey, Columbus. He made you laugh, and your laughter made me happy. And so I let you in."

"Thank you, Columbus!" shouted the children, patting the little donkey. "Thank you ever so much."

"Listen," said the master of the house, holding up his hand for quiet. "I have just had a wonderful idea. Each day, from now on, I shall leave my gate open so that you can come into the yard and play. And whenever the cabinet-maker and his little donkey come to town, we will have lunch on the lawn as we did today."

At this, the children jumped up and down and clapped their hands and the old cabinet-maker went over and put his arms about Columbus' neck and gave him a big hug.

When the last child had scampered out through the great iron gates, Columbus' master hitched him to the donkey cart, said good-by to the man on the porch, and started off toward home, feeling happier than he ever had before.

The little donkey was happy too. It had been a wonderful day for him, and he shook his bell gaily as he trotted along over the country roads. But after a while he slackened his pace. And then he came to a full stop. He had reached the shady lane that he had so long wanted to explore. What if he went in there now? he wondered. Would his master stop him?

"All right, Columbus," the old cabinet-maker said with a laugh. "You deserve a little treat as a reward for the way you behaved today. You made a good many people happy because you sang at just the right time. So go ahead and enjoy yourself. Butterfly Brook will be there when we get back."

Without waiting a moment, Columbus crossed the road and turned in at the shady lane. And this time there was no jerk on the lines to stop him!

*By Alice Crew Gall and Fleming Crew*

## THE GOLDFISH

THE FIRST THING Mrs. Harman saw when she opened the nursery door was the cat crouched upon the table, tense and motionless, watching Peter, the goldfish, in his glass bowl.

"Shoo! You're a bad cat! Shoo!" she cried, stamping her foot.

The cat shot her a quick, guilty glance, and was gone like a shadow through the doorway.

"Shoo!" cried Mrs. Harman after her, and turned to her son.

"You shouldn't let the cat in here, Don. She'll get Peter."

Seven-year-old Don was seated on the floor struggling with a shoe lace.

"Now—" he began, "now—I didn't see her, Mother. I've been tying my laces. Mother, will you telephone for Craig to come over and play? You know I was disappointed yesterday and day before, and— Will you, Mother?"

"Have you spotted today?" asked Mrs. Harman.

"A little jelly spot at lunch. It was very little, and— now—I didn't spot at breakfast."

"Very well," said Mrs. Harman, "I'll see if Craig can come."

But Craig could not come and for the third successive day Don was disappointed.

"You see it's near Christmas, dear," the mother explained, "and all the boys are busy."

"I'm not busy," Don told her wistfully.

"I'll tell you what you can do." Mrs. Harman spoke brightly. "You can write a letter to Santa Claus. Won't that be fun? It's only three weeks to Christmas, and he'll be wondering what you want."

"I don't know what I want." His tone was listless.

"Snow shoes?" she suggested.

"Oh, I don't know."

"A sled?"

Don brightened. The sled gave him an idea.

"I know what. I want a brother. Not a little one. A regular brother. Big, you know, with lots and lots of teeth."

"They're hard to get in those large sizes," Mrs. Harman said, "and it's so near Christmas they must be pretty well picked over. The best plan is to write to Santa about it. Here's paper with lines, and a nice sharp pencil."

Don sat down at his little desk and in a round laborious hand began to write. The letter, when completed, ran uphill and down and read as follows:

> Dear Santy
>    i am well i hope you are well i would like a boy with teeth the biggest one you can spair for a brother
>                    yours truly
>                    D Harman

The paper, originally white, was changed to gray in the process of writing, and smudges had somehow been communicated to Don's face and hands.

"Now," said his mother, "we'll send it."

"Do you think he'll get it tonight?"

"He ought to."

They moved to the fireplace; Mrs. Harman touched a match to the letter and they watched it burn to a black, wavering crisp, and disappear.

That night Mrs. Harman told her husband she was worried about Don.

"He needs boys to play with," she said.

"There seem to be plenty of boys in the neighborhood," Mr. Harman replied.

"Yes, but they're not his age. Craig is Don's age but he lives almost a mile away, and Don doesn't see much of him except at school. I was thinking—" She sighed and broke off.

"What were you thinking, dear?"

"I was thinking of little Fred, your sister Helen's boy. He's just three months older than Don, you know."

"Isn't he getting on all right at Aunt Henrietta's?"

"I suppose so. But your Aunt Henrietta is growing old, and—well, it's not as if he had a father and a mother."

"Look here, Sallie," her husband said, "you've got something in your mind. What is it? Do you feel that we ought to—" He did not finish the question, for his wife was nodding at him, smiling.

Meanwhile, up in the nursery, Don was eating his supper and his nurse was watching every mouthful.

"Will you never learn to be a little gentleman?" she demanded. "Look at your napkin. One mass of jelly. I'll have to show it to your mother. A big boy like you, and Christmas so near, too!"

"I don't care," said Don, defiantly.

"One mass of jelly," she repeated. "I'll certainly have to show it to your mother." So saying, she took the offending napkin from the boy's neck and left the room.

"I don't care!" he said again, and moved slowly over to the table where, with chin on hands, he sat and gazed at Peter, the goldfish, in his bowl.

He was not thinking of the bowl; he was not staring into it as the cat had stared, but through it at something far beyond—just what, I do not know. Nor do I know how long he sat there gazing beyond the glass and the water and the weeds and the little castle and even Peter himself. It may have been a long time or a short time, but whether it was long or short his attention was at last attracted by a tiny squeaky sound.

He listened and the sound grew plainer. Somehow it

suggested words—words which at first seemed to come from so far away you couldn't understand them. Then suddenly he realized that the sound was coming from inside the goldfish bowl.

Don looked at Peter. He was not swimming now, but was lying motionless, nose pressed against the glass, staring out into the nursery. His mouth was moving. It opened and shut, opened and shut, and the squeaky little sound continued.

Don leaned forward and turned one ear to the bowl. The sound grew plainer.

"Is that you, Peter?"

"Yes! Yes! Yes! Yes!" the little squeak responded instantly.

"Don't talk so fast," said Don. "What do you want?"

"Help me out!"

"All right," said the boy, but when he dipped his hand into the water, Peter darted to his castle.

"Not like that! You'll drown me!"

"You can't drown a fish."

"Have you ever been a fish?" asked Peter sharply.

"Of course not."

"Then what do you know about it?"

"I'm a boy, and a boy knows more than a fish."

"He thinks he does!" As Peter spoke, four round bubbles issued from his mouth and followed one another to the surface, where they broke with a chuckling sound: "Ha-ha-ha-ha!"

Don did not like to be laughed at by grown-ups, let alone fish.

"If that's how you're going to talk," he said, "I won't help you."

"Wait a minute! I want to tell you something. Will you promise not to tell?"

"Yes, what?"

"Put your ear close."

Don hesitated. "No tricks, now! If you jump up and nip my ear, or yell in it, or anything like that, I'll grab you out and have you cooked."

Peter looked shocked. "I wouldn't think of playing tricks on you," he said. "May I float belly-up if I would."

"Well, go ahead, then."

"I'm ashamed to tell it." The little fish looked very red. "It happened through my messy way of eating. They all warned me—my mother, my aunt, my nurse —but I—"

"Your nurse? Fish don't have nurses."

"That was before I *was* a fish. It was when I was a boy."

"Were you a boy?" Don was hardly able to believe his ears.

"Yes."

"What happened to you?"

"Spilling did it—spilling food on my napkin and the tablecloth."

"A fish hasn't napkins and tablecloths."

"Of course not; that's just it," said Peter. "That's how I happened to become a fish. They told me I didn't deserve a napkin on a lap. They told me I ought to be

kept in water. But I never dreamed I'd come to this."
A little groan came from the bowl.

"Don't you like to be a fish?" asked Don. "You don't
have to go to school."

"Swimming was fun at first," said Peter, "but I'm
awfully tired of it. The bowl's so round—one side just
like another. And when my nose tickles I miss my hands
terribly. Really there's nothing as nice as being a boy
with hands and a clean white napkin and a lap."

"I wish I could get you out," said Don, "but you'd
flip around on the table and die, wouldn't you?"

"Yes, there's only one way to turn me back into a
boy."

"How?"

"Another boy must do it for me. He has to keep his
napkin clean for a week."

"A whole *week?*" Don gasped.

"Only a week. After that I'll be his brother. I can
make box kites, and we could dig caves, and keep rabbits, and get some garter snakes, and some—"

"I'll try!" exclaimed Don. "I'll try like everything!"

"Oh, thanks!" said Peter. "I can't tell you what it's
going to mean to me!" He looked through the other side
of the bowl at the calendar on the wall. "This is the
seventeenth. You begin tomorrow morning. You only
have to keep your napkin clean until the twenty-fourth,
and then—why, my scales! That will be Christmas Eve!
How jolly!"

"If I should spot just once," Don asked, "would that
spoil everything?"

Peter quivered.

"Don't speak of such a thing!" he begged. "And remember, you are not to breathe a word of what I've told you. If you tell, the whole thing will be—"

"There you are!" cried the nurse, appearing in the doorway. "You're supposed to be in bed. Now, I'll have to tell your mother."

Don turned and blinked at her. Then he arose, shuffled over to his bed, slipped out of his bathrobe and tumbled in.

The week dragged along. The Christmas preparations, the mysterious packages, the crackling of wrapping paper Don heard through the closed door of his mother's room—none of these things occupied his mind as they had the year before. His thoughts were fixed on the tremendous task of freeing Peter. Somehow, somehow he must manage to keep his napkin spotless for a week. He must!

At first he thought the safest plan would be to go without meals altogether; but when he tried it Nurse scolded, and besides he got hungry. His one idea when he sat down to eat was to keep from splattering and spilling. When there was meat with gravy he cut it into little pieces with the utmost care, never allowing his knife or fork to slip. He spread his apple sauce and jelly very thin upon his bread and butter, and saw to it that none was hanging to the edges. He pushed his glass of water or milk far back from the table's edge, and when he drank he took the smallest swallows. As for cereals, eggs and soft, custardy desserts, he ate such little spoonfuls that Nurse could not believe her eyes, and wondered "what ailed the child."

To his surprise he found the task less difficult as meals and days went by. There were little tricks, he learned, to keep from making spots, and the more you practiced them the better you got. But as the work grew easier, responsibility increased. It would be awful to dribble something on his napkin after having kept it clean three days . . . four days . . . five days.

When Nurse was absent from the room he would go to Peter's bowl and whisper reassuring words; but Peter never spoke again, although he looked at Don with sad, appealing eyes, especially during meals.

At breakfast on the seventh day Peter was plainly nervous. At luncheon he was more excited still. And when night came his fins and tail were all a-quiver as he gazed through the glass wall.

This made it hard for Don. He tried not to watch Peter. At lunch he made a slip with some potato but caught it in his hand before it reached his napkin. As this occurred, a great big bubble rose like a sigh from Peter's mouth.

Having safely disposed of the last spoonful of custard, Don gave a joyful cry. He removed his napkin, and raised it like a fair white banner.

"Look!" he cried. "A whole week, and not a single spot!"

"Now, I do declare!" exclaimed the nurse, who thought he was showing it to her. "How good little boys do get when Christmas is coming. It shows what you can do. Look at it, all clean and white! I'll have to show it to your mother." She took the napkin and left the room.

Don placed his elbows on the table, rested his chin in his hands, and gazed intently at the goldfish bowl.

"Peter!" he whispered softly.

But Peter only swam about, as much a goldfish as he ever was.

Don was disappointed. He had hoped the thing would happen after supper, while Nurse was there. He had imagined Peter rising from the water, changing shape, and dropping off his scales—until he stood a full-fledged boy. How Nurse's eyes would bulge! But though this didn't happen, Don never lost his faith; he only sat there wondering how and when the change would come.

"There you are!" cried the nurse, appearing in the doorway. "You're supposed to be in bed. Now, I'll have to go and tell your mother."

Don skipped over to the bed and leaped in.

"You such a big boy," Nurse went on, "and this Christmas Eve, and your stocking hanging in the living room! I'll really have to tell your mother." She was muttering and puttering around the nursery as he fell asleep.

"Shoo! Shoo! You bad cat!" It was Mrs. Harman's voice.

Don turned over in his bed and squinted at the early morning light.

"Merry Christmas, dear!"

"Merry Christmas, Mother!" He sat up suddenly and stared with wide eyes at the goldfish bowl.

"Why, Peter's gone!" he cried, jumping out of bed.

"Never mind that now," said his mother. "You must hurry down and see all the lovely things Santa left in the living room. Get into your bathrobe and slippers. Hurry, son!"

As she spoke Don heard a motor in the driveway. Then the slam of the front door and his father's voice in the hall below.

"Dad! Dad!" he shouted, rushing down the stairs.

On the bottom step he stopped abruptly. There, holding tightly to his father's hand, stood another boy, a boy just Don's size. He grinned, and as he did so Don saw that he had lots and lots of teeth.

The two stared at each other for a moment. Then Don moved slowly forward.

"We can make box kites," he said, "and dig caves, and keep rabbits and—"

"And garter snakes," put in the other boy.

—Condensed by Permission of the Author

*By Julian Street*

## THE BEAN BOY

IN THE YEARS between this and that, there lived a little boy named String, because he used strings for shoelaces: a red string in one shoe and a green string in the other. Now, String lived in a Lima bean field. And when the Lima beans were green he picked them, put them in sacks, and took sackfuls of green Lima beans into town to sell, so he was called the Bean Boy.

One morning, when the town looked yellow and dusty as a Chinaman sitting in the sun, String stopped at the Governor's Palace to leave a sack of green Lima beans for the Governor's little daughter, who had ordered large, flat beans in her soup. She was called Dulce because, although her eyes were dark and sad, her smile was sweet and gaudy as a dulce.

Now, Dulce was leaning out of the palace window watching for her sack of large, flat beans, when the Bean Boy came whistling into the patio of the palace, tripping over his red and green shoestrings, always coming undone. Dulce ran downstairs, fetching a pan, so the Bean Boy could dump out his sack of big, flat beans. Then the Bean Boy sat down to tie up his green and red shoestrings. By this time, the Governor's little daughter had stopped smiling, so String noticed how sad and dark her eyes looked.

"It must be nice," she said, "to live in a bean field and bring sacks of beans into town."

"It is nice. And I am always finding things on the way in and out."

"What kind of things?" asked Dulce eagerly.

"Oh, tree toads and moonstones and old Spanish pesos and Indian beads and kelp for dress-up helmets."

At that the Governor's little daughter smiled her gaudy smile.

"Maybe," she asked, "maybe you can find my dream for me?"

"Maybe I can," said the Bean Boy.

"I dreamed," Dulce said, "that my father was not a governor any more and didn't need to worry about revolutions. I dreamed that he was an organ-grinder man, with a tiny tomboy monkey from Central America."

The Bean Boy nodded. "I know. And you went with him, walking through bean fields, singing 'Maria Mia.'

And people filled your cup with pennies. And you made a bonfire every night, popping stacks of corn."

"Yes, yes, and my father didn't worry any more about revolutions. Just think, he didn't need to worry about revolutions."

Dulce opened her sad eyes wide open. "But I only dreamed it once. Now, do you think you can find my dream again for me?"

"Of course." And the Bean Boy took a moonstone, an Indian bead, a tree toad, and an old Spanish coin out of his pocket, spreading them on the tile floor in front of Dulce.

"Of course," said the Bean Boy. "I can find anything on my way in and out."

"Then," said Dulce, "I intend to marry you when you grow up tall."

At that the Bean Boy went whistling away, tying up the green and red strings, always coming undone.

Next morning at sunup, String was picking big, flat beans and putting them into sacks, when a Goblin came hurrying up a bean row and tipped his bean-leaf cap, stuck round with oak holly berries, green and red ones.

"Could you possibly spare two good-sized beans this morning?" the Goblin inquired politely. "The finest baby of our king will be christened in sixteen minutes, and I find myself without a christening present."

The polite Goblin bowed as best he could, for he was a thick little person. He had a wide, cheerful mouth and looked hearty in his seaweed suit.

The Bean Boy was red with surprise.

"Two beans, you want two beans!" he kept saying.

"If you can spare them, please," said the polite Goblin.

"Fill your cap," String told him. And he helped the Goblin pick eight or ten fine Lima beans.

"While you are here," the Bean Boy said hurriedly, "I wish you would tell me where to find the dream of the Governor's little girl, Dulce."

The polite Goblin bowed in spite of his girth. "Certainly," he said, "all dreams are kept in the Cave of Yawns down by the sea, two leagues south, two leagues west. And there you are. But remember not to yawn in the cave. For every time anyone yawns, the cave gets bigger and bigger, opening up at the end. And if you go to sleep in there, you will never wake up. Then," asked the Goblin, "who will pick the beans, put them in sacks, and take sacksful of Lima beans into town?"

He went away, looking surprised at his own question.

At that the Bean Boy hurried off, going two leagues south, two leagues west. And there he was at the Cave of Yawns down by the sea. There were dark chests along the walls of the cave. Rich, hand-carved chests, out of which the Sandman was selecting dreams. He stood at the farthest end of the cave, throwing a handful of sand into his bag and then a dream. Just like that—a handful of sand and then a dream. "Whoo, whoo," called the Bean Boy, but when the Sandman looked up the Bean Boy yawned.

The cave opened up at the end just as the polite Goblin said it would. The Sandman was leagues farther away now than he had been before.

The Bean Boy began to feel sleepy now. His hands went to sleep, his feet went to sleep, and every step pricked like pins and needles. Then the Bean Boy yawned again, and the cave opened up at the end, just as the polite Goblin said it would. The Sandman and the rich, hand-carved chests were so far away now they looked like dots on a dotted line. Then the Bean Boy's ears went to sleep. After that his nose went to sleep. But he said to himself, "Even though I feel all over like a pincushion, I must keep my two eyes awake and walk with my feet asleep until I can nudge the Sandman and get Dulce's dream for her."

So the Bean Boy walked with his feet asleep, his hands asleep, his ears asleep, and his nose asleep. But the jolt of tripping over his shoestrings kept his eyes awake, until he nudged the Sandman.

"Please," he said stifling an enormous yawn, "may I have Dulce's dream?"

"What was it like?" asked the Sandman. "And about how long?"

"Hurry," cried the Bean Boy, "I'm going to yawn again."

"Did it have a monkey and an organ grinder in it and a song called 'Maria Mia'?"

"Yes, yes." The Bean Boy's eyes were closing. But he tripped over his shoestrings and opened them again with a terrible effort.

"It's an old dream," said the Sandman, "almost worn out, so I suppose you may as well have it." He shook the dream out, sticking his finger through the holes. The Bean Boy's eyes closed again. He shook himself,

saying, "My hands are asleep, my feet are asleep, and
so are my nose and ears, but though I feel like a pincushion all over, I must keep my eyes open." So he
opened his eyes. The Sandman handed him the old,
tattered dream, and the Bean Boy ran from the cave
with his feet asleep, his hands asleep, his ears asleep,
and his nose asleep. He was really asleep all over, except that his eyes were awake from the jolt of tripping
over his shoestrings, a red string in one shoe and a green
string in the other.

Next morning, before dawn, the little boy started for
town with his bean sacks and the old dream, which
looked as if it were falling to pieces. When he came
near the gates of the town, he heard guns. At that, soldiers came out, singing lustily, "Maria Mia." The Bean
Boy went into town. The palace was in ruins, and there
on some stones sat the Governor and Dulce.

"We have had another revolution," Dulce told the
Bean Boy, who noticed how sad and dark her eyes were.

Just then a soldier came running up and spoke low
to the Governor.

"Your Excellency must go away at once in disguise!"

Whereupon the Bean Boy handed Dulce the old worn
dream.

And so it happened that the Governor disguised himself as an organ-grinder man, owning a tiny tomboy
monkey from Central America. He and Dulce and the
Bean Boy wandered up and down the world joyously,
making bonfires every night and popping stacks of corn.
After they had wandered from one end of the world to

the other, the Bean Boy married Dulce one night by a
big campfire, and they inherited great stretches of bean
fields, where they lived happily for years and years and
years and years.

*By Monica Shannon*

# THE BROWNIE IN THE HOUSE

## O PROVIDENCE!

When all the world was young and green,
And babies grew, the rocks between,
  And slumbered in the shade;
Then fox and hen and cat and mouse;
All dwelt together in one house,
  And had one serving maid.—
O Providence, O Providence, why must such pictures
  fade?

In those good days the brownie-men
Were digging gold in every glen,
  And slept on every bough;
For her who kept her house aright

172

They washed and scrubbed and made things bright,
    I cannot tell you how.—
O Providence, O Providence, where are the brownies
        now?

IN THOSE DAYS, when the fox and the cock were bosom
friends, there lived a man at the edge of the green forest
who had one fair daughter, and no child else. The
mother was dead some time since, and the father and
daughter lived all alone, but for all that they prospered
exceedingly, and life was for them as smooth as new
butter. There was a sound enough reason for all this:
there was a brownie in that house, and to say that is
almost as much as to clink the money between one's
fingers.

The daughter got out of bed at four o'clock, and
baked and brewed and spun and sewed; the father went
out into the wood and gathered faggots, and came back to
his own dooryard and planted turnips. Every night the
daughter took a fresh bowl, and put steaming porridge
in it, with a lump of butter as big as a goose egg floating
on the top, and set it by the hearth; in the morning she
found the pans scoured so that she could see her face in
them, the good bread was ready for the oven, and the
yarn was piled in heaps for the weaver; the faggots
were trimmed, and the turnips were gathered and
washed and left in a basin. And the bowl was empty on
the hearth. So they had padded pockets and light
hearts; but Luck lays no eggs if her throat is cut, and
so the man found out. You shall hear:

One time the farmer went to the town to trade, and
was gone three days and a day; when he came back, he

had a wife with him, and a new daughter to boot, for he had married a widow with a daughter of her own. The woman was as gentle as a breeze in summer, and the stepsister was a good-looking body, and pleasant-spoken enough, but from that day there was nothing but curdled cream in that house. The daughter worked as hard as ever, but she got no help from the stepsister, who sat with her hands folded and counted the flies on the wall. And as for the bowl on the hearth: scraps from the kitchen with a lump of fat on top were good enough for any brownie—that was what the stepmother said.

After that, when the daughter came into the kitchen at four o'clock, she found the pans rusted and black, the good bread flat and lumpy, and the yarn tangled and torn; the faggots were scattered on the floor, and the turnips were left where they were gathered. So the poor girl had to work twice as hard as ever she had before, with no more thanks than the bees gave the bear when they found him stealing honey; but she cared less for that than she did for the good brownie, who was cheated of his due as the luck of the house.

Well, the time came when the daughter could stand it no longer; so one night at the first cock-crow, when all the household was asleep, she went into the kitchen and poked the fire into a blaze, for she was going to make porridge for the brownie, say what they might.

"Tut! tut!" says one among the ashes, "and what do you here, troublemaker?" And out pops the brownie in his red cap, with ashes in his whiskers and his furry ears.

"Hush!" says the daughter of the house; "tongues were made for other things besides talking! I crave your pardon for disturbing your rest, but I have porridge to make." The brownie cut a caper, as merry as a red leaf in the October wind; and the maiden took a blue bowl, and after she had mixed the porridge, she put it in the bowl with a wooden spoon and a lump of butter as big as a goose egg, and set it in the ingle. Then she was all for hurrying away without a look over her shoulder, for the good little people have no love of those who spy upon them; but the brownie waved his wooden spoon at her, and snorted, that being the only sound he could make, since his mouth was crammed with porridge.

"Come back!" says he presently; "that is an ill master who gives a horse nothing but straw. Look you, if a traveler passes by this way, and offers you aught from his store, do you make free to ask for that which pleases you."

So the maid thanked the brownie as gravely as if he had given her a ring with rubies in it; but then, she had not put chips in that basket in hopes of finding them turned into guldens—so she was perfectly satisfied.

The next day the pans were scoured so that one would have said they were golden, the good bread was sweet and freshly kneaded, and the yarn was rolled in skeins ready for the weaving; the faggots were trimmed, and the turnips were washed and left in a basin. And the bowl was empty on the hearth. The daughter put it away and said nothing about it; and every night thereafter she crept into the kitchen and set the porridge in the ingle.

Well, it was but a short time afterward that the house-father must needs stumble over a pile of faggots and sprain his ankle; and now the daughter must go to town and do the trading, for the other two were needed at home. So off she set with a basket on her arm, as neat and fresh as a meadow daisy; and while she was gone the stepsister was to do the work she attended to when she was at home.

Dear me! what a stir Lazy-bones made about it! She did no more than peel the turnips and wash the pots, but the cat by the fire could have done as well, and with less grumbling. The turnips were boiled to shreds, the cloth was set on the table awry, and the pots were hung on the first nail she saw, with streaks of grease and soot upon them.

That night, about the first cock-crow, the stepsister woke with a squeak, for she thought somebody was pinching her. Sure enough, her arms were the color of blackberries and smoke, and they kept on growing darker and darker and sorer and sorer, for the pinches came as fast and thick as raindrops in a thunderstorm. She rolled out of bed, and laid about her smartly with her shoe, but all to no avail; and suddenly there came a noise from the kitchen that sounded as if a regiment of soldiers were fighting with bayonets. Such a clashing and rattling was never heard since the last time the hill opened and showed the little men of the mountains hammering at their forges.

The stepsister crept to the kitchen door and peered

in. There was the brownie on the table, with his red cap all askew, hurling the dirty pots about, and laughing like a mad March hare. "Ah, there you are, Soggyhead," says he; "now perhaps you will be washing the pots clean, since I have been good enough to get them down for you!"

The stepsister was all for saying no, but there are times when wisdom leads to courage, as the fox said when he jumped through the back window of the henhouse as the farmer came in at the door. Willy-nilly, she picked up the dirty pans and set about scouring them, for whenever she stopped to rest, the pinches began again harder than ever. By the time the red sun came marching over the hill, the last pan was scoured, but the brownie had swung himself up on the smokejack, and gone up the chimney, so that all Lady Heavyfoot had for her labor was a pair of dirty hands and hollows under the eyes. And here was the daughter home from the town, and tapping at the door.

Three days thereafter, there came a traveler with a pack to the door of the house on the green forest-edge. He was dressed in a dusty brown jerkin, and ragged woolen hose, and his cloak was as much protection against the weather as a bit of gossamer; but his face was brown and keen, and there was that in it which made the daughter of the house think to herself, "Oh, if only the saints would send me such a one!"

And was there a bite and a sup for a foot-weary man? That was what the traveler asked. The stepmother looked askance at his ragged clothes, but at last she said yes, there was, and set before the traveler a bowl of broken bits that were about to be thrown to the dogs.

"Is there no better than that, sister?" said the daughter of the house.

"Suppose there is?" said the stepsister; "it is not my place to wait on beggars."

So the daughter waited until the stepmother had gone, and then she took away the bowl of scraps. She went over to the bin where the flour was, and took a bit of the brown flour, and a drop of water, and began to stir them together; and the more she stirred the whiter it got. So then she poked up the fire, and set the cake over it; and it puffed up, light and toothsome, and fit for a Prince's eating. This she offered to the traveler, with a cup of milk and a square of cheese.

"Thanks is a thin word when the heart is full," says the traveler. "Is there nothing I can give you out of my poor store?" And he opened the pack.

Hi! you should have seen the stepsister's eyes stand out then! For the pack was full of jewels and gold, and rings and chains and armlets without number. But the daughter shook her head at them.

"I am free to ask for what I want," says she to herself, "but I have no right surely to any of these, for by them the traveler earns his bread, and he has need of them." So at last all she asked for was the bit of brown cord that was hanging about his neck.

The traveler took off the cord, and on the end of it was a little rusty key; he threw it over her head, and the key was rusty no more, but as bright as the King's crown. "That is the key to the treasure house of joy," says he, "and you and I will go and find the door of it together."

"But is there nothing for me?" said the stepsister.

"Take what you like," says the traveler. Well, the sister looked and looked, and fingered one thing after another; and at last she seized a great ring with red fiery stones in it, and put it on. Behold! it was changed to a gray toadstool, that grew tight to her finger, and could not be got off; and she wore it all the days of her life.

"Nothing for nothing," said the traveler. So then he took the daughter by the hand, and they went out of the door together; the sun was warm upon their faces, for it was the first of summertime.

But after that time the brownie was never seen in that house any more, and they had no more good fortune than a cricket in the winter snow. And have you never seen a brownie? Well, do you get up at four o'clock, and bake and brew and spin and sew, and perhaps if you come into the kitchen at the first cock-crow some night, you will find him swinging on the smoke-jack.

*By Margery Bailey*

## ROCKING-HORSE LAND

LITTLE PRINCE FREEDLING woke up with a jump, and
sprang out of bed into the sunshine. He was five years
old that morning, by all the clocks and calendars in the
kingdom; and the day was going to be beautiful. Every
golden minute was precious. He was dressed and out of
his room before the attendants knew that he was awake.

In the ante-chamber stood piles on piles of glittering
presents; when he walked among them they came up to
the measure of his waist. His fairy godmother had sent
him a toy with the most humorous effect. It was labeled,
"Break me and I shall turn into something else." So
every time he broke it he got a new toy more beautiful
than the last. It began by being a hoop, and from that it
ran on, while the Prince broke it incessantly for the
space of one hour, during which it became by turn—a
top, a Noah's ark, a skipping-rope, a man-of-war, a box
of bricks, a picture puzzle, a pair of stilts, a drum, a

trumpet, a kaleidoscope, a steam-engine, and nine hundred and fifty other things exactly. Then he began to grow discontented, because it would never turn into the same thing again; and after having broken the man-of-war he wanted to get it back again. Also he wanted to see if the steam-engine would go inside the Noah's ark; but the toy would never be two things at the same time, either. This was very unsatisfactory. He thought his fairy godmother ought to have sent him two toys, out of which he could make combinations.

At last he broke it once more, and it turned into a kite; and while he was flying the kite he broke the string, and the kite went sailing away up into nasty blue sky, and was never heard of again.

Then Prince Freedling sat down and howled at his fairy godmother; what a dissembling lot fairy godmothers were, to be sure! They were always setting traps to make their god-children unhappy. Nevertheless, when told to, he took up his pen and wrote her a nice little note, full of bad spelling and tarradiddles, to say what a happy birthday he was spending in breaking up the beautiful toy she had sent him.

Then he went to look at the rest of the presents, and found it quite refreshing to break a few that did not send him giddy by turning into anything else.

Suddenly his eyes became fixed with delight; alone, right at the end of the room, stood a great black rocking-horse. The saddle and bridle were hung with tiny gold bells and balls of coral; and the horse's tail and mane flowed till they almost touched the ground.

The Prince scampered across the room, and threw his

arms around the beautiful creature's neck. All its bells jangled as the head swayed gracefully down; and the Prince kissed it between the eyes. Great eyes they were, the color of fire; so wonderfully bright, it seemed they must be really alive; only they did not move, but gazed continually with a set stare at the tapestry-hung wall, on which were figures of armed knights riding to battle.

So Prince Freedling mounted to the back of his rocking-horse; and all day long he rode and shouted to the figures of the armed knights, challenging them to fight, or leading them against the enemy.

At length, when it came to be bedtime, weary of so much glory, he was lifted down from the saddle and carried away to bed.

In his sleep Freedling still felt his black rocking-horse swinging to and fro under him, and heard the melodious chime of its bells, and, in the land of dreams, saw a great country open before him, full of the sound of the battle-cry and the hunting-horn calling him to strange perils and triumphs.

In the middle of the night he grew softly awake, and his heart was full of love for his black rocking-horse. He crept gently out of bed: he would go and look at it where it was standing so grand and still in the next room, to make sure that it was all safe and not afraid of being by itself in the dark night. Parting the door-hangings he passed through into the wide hollow chamber beyond, all littered about with toys.

The moon was shining in through the window, making a square cistern of light upon the floor. And then, all at once, he saw that the rocking-horse had moved from the place where he had left it! It had crossed the room, and was standing close to the window, with its head toward the night, as though watching the movement of the clouds and the trees swaying in the wind.

The Prince could not understand how it had been moved so; he was a little bit afraid and, stealing timidly across, he took hold of the bridle to comfort himself with the jangle of its bells. As he came close, and looked up into the dark solemn face, he saw that the eyes were full of tears and, reaching up, felt one fall warm against his hand.

"Why do you weep, my Beautiful?" said the Prince.

The rocking-horse answered, "I weep because I am a prisoner, and not free. Open the window, Master, and let me go!"

"But if I let you go I shall lose you," said the Prince. "Cannot you be happy here with me?"

"Let me go," said the horse, "for my brothers call me out of Rocking-Horse Land; I hear my mare whinnying to her foals; and they all cry, seeking me through the ups and hollows of my native fastness! Sweet Master, let me go this night, and I will return to you when it is day!"

Then Freedling said, "How shall I know that you will return; and what name shall I call you by?"

And the rocking-horse answered, "My name is Rollonde. Search my mane till you find in it a white hair; draw it out and wind it upon one of your fingers; and as long as you have it so wound you are my master; and wherever I am I must return at your bidding."

So the Prince drew down the rocking-horse's head;

and searching the mane, he found the white hair, and wound it upon his finger and tied it. Then he kissed Rollonde between the eyes, saying, "Go, Rollonde, since I love you, and wish you to be happy; only return to me when it is day!" And so saying, he threw open the window to the stir of the night.

Then the rocking-horse lifted his dark head and neighed aloud for joy, and swaying forward with a mighty circling motion rose full into the air, and sprang out into the free world before him.

Freedling watched how with plunge and curve he went over the bowed trees; and again he neighed into the darkness of the night, then swifter than wind disappeared in the distance. And faintly from far away came a sound of the neighing of many horses answering him.

Then the Prince closed the window and crept back to bed; and all night long he dreamed strange dreams of Rocking-Horse Land. There he saw smooth hills and valleys that rose and sank without a stone or a tree to disturb the steel-like polish of their surface, slippery as glass, and driven over by a strong wind; and over them, with a sound like the humming of bees, flew the rocking-horses. Up and down, up and down, with bright manes streaming like colored fires, and feet motionless behind and before, went the swift pendulum of their flight. Their long bodies bowed and rose; their heads worked to give impetus to their going; they cried, neighing to each other over hill and valley, "Which of us shall be first? Which of us shall be first?" After them the mares with their tall foals came spinning to watch, crying also among themselves, "Ah! which shall be first?"

"Rollonde, Rollonde is first!" shouted the Prince, clapping his hands as they reached the goal; and at that, all at once, he woke, and saw it was broad day. Then he ran and threw open the window and, holding out the finger that carried the white hair, cried, "Rollonde, Rollonde, come back, Rollonde!"

Far away he heard an answering sound; and in another moment there came the great rocking-horse himself, dipping and dancing over the hills. He crossed the woods and cleared the palace-wall at a bound, and floating in through the window, dropped to rest at Prince Freedling's side, rocking gently to and fro as though panting from the strain of his long flight.

"Now are you happy?" asked the Prince as he caressed him.

"Ah! sweet Prince," said Rollonde, "ah, kind Master!" And then he said no more, but became the stock-still, staring rocking-horse of the day before, with fixed eyes and rigid limbs, which could do nothing but rock up and down with a jangling of sweet bells so long as the Prince rode him.

That night Freedling came again when all was still in the palace; and now as before Rollonde had moved from his place and was standing with his head against the window waiting to be let out. "Ah, dear Master," he said, as soon as he saw the Prince coming, "let me go this night also, and surely I will return with day."

So again the Prince opened the window, and watched him disappear, and heard from far away the neighing of the horses in Rocking-Horse Land calling to him. And in the morning, with the white hair round his finger, he called, "Rollonde, Rollonde!" and Rollonde neighed and came back to him, dipping and dancing over the hills.

Now this same thing happened every night; and every morning the horse kissed Freedling, saying, "Ah! dear Prince and kind Master!" and became stock-still once more.

So a year went by, till one morning Freedling woke up to find it was his sixth birthday. And as six is to five, so were the presents he received on his sixth birthday for magnificence and multitude to the presents he had received the year before. His fairy godmother had sent him a bird, a real live bird; but when he pulled its tail it became a lizard, and when he pulled the lizard's tail it became a mouse, and when he pulled the mouse's tail it became a cat. Then he did very much want to see if the cat would eat the mouse, and not being able to have them both he got rather vexed with his fairy godmother. However, he pulled the cat's tail and the cat became a dog, and when he pulled the dog's tail the dog became a goat; and so it went on till he got to a cow. And he pulled the cow's tail and it became a camel, and he pulled the camel's tail and it became an elephant, and still not being contented, he pulled the elephant's tail and it became a guinea-pig. Now a guinea-pig has no tail to pull, so it remained a guinea-pig, while Prince Freedling sat down and howled at his fairy godmother.

But the best of all his presents was the one given to

him by the King his father. It was a most beautiful horse, for, said the King, "You are now old enough to learn to ride."

So Freedling was put upon the horse's back, and from having ridden so long upon his rocking-horse he learned to ride perfectly in a single day, and was declared by all the courtiers to be the most perfect equestrian that was ever seen.

Now these praises and the pleasure of riding a real horse so occupied his thoughts that that night he forgot all about Rollonde, and falling fast asleep dreamed of nothing but real horses and horsemen going to battle. And so it was the next night too.

But the night after that, just as he was falling asleep, he heard someone sobbing by his bed, and a voice saying, "Ah! dear Prince and kind Master, let me go, for my heart breaks for a sight of my native land." And there stood his poor rocking-horse Rollonde, with tears falling out of his beautiful eyes on to the white coverlet.

Then the Prince, full of shame at having forgotten his friend, sprang up and threw his arms round his neck, saying, "Be of good cheer, Rollonde, for now surely I will let thee go!" and he ran to the window and opened it for the horse to go through. "Ah! dear Prince and kind Master!" said Rollonde. Then he lifted his head and neighed so that the whole palace shook; and swaying forward till his head almost touched the ground, he sprang out into the night and away toward Rocking-Horse Land.

Then Prince Freedling, standing by the window, thoughtfully unloosed the white hair from his finger, and let it float away into the darkness, out of sight of his eye or reach of his hand.

"Good-by, Rollonde," he murmured softly, "brave Rollonde, my own good Rollonde! Go and be happy in your own land, since I, your Master, was forgetting to be kind to you." And far away he heard the neighing of horses in Rocking-Horse Land.

Many years after, when Freedling had become King in his father's stead, the fifth birthday of the Prince his son came to be celebrated; and there on the morning of the day, among all the presents that covered the floor of the chamber, stood a beautiful foal rocking-horse, black, with deep-burning eyes.

No one knew how it had come there, or whose present it was, till the King himself came to look at it. And when he saw it so like the old Rollonde he had loved as a boy, he smiled, and, stroking its dark mane, said softly in its ear, "Art thou, then, the son of Rollonde?" And the foal answered him, "Ah, dear Prince and kind Master!" but never a word more.

Then the King took the little Prince his son, and told him the story of Rollonde as I have told it here; and at the end he went and searched in the foal's mane till he found one white hair, and, drawing it out, he wound it about the little Prince's finger, bidding him guard it well and be ever a kind master to Rollonde's son.

So here is my story of Rollonde come to a good ending.

*By Laurence Housman*

## IF YOU HAD A WISH?

IN THE OLD DAYS, and very good days they were (this was in France long ago), there was a fisherman, and never did hard-working, cheerful fellow have worse luck. If a storm blew up it was his nets that were carried away. If he caught no fish the market would be good, and if he caught a good haul there would be no market at all. Yet he was a cheerful soul who never complained, even when his wife, a sour-tempered woman, scolded and frowned.

"I see nothing to smile for," she would say when he came home empty-handed. "You bring nothing with as merry a look as if you had a boatful."

"Why not sing?" he would reply. "The longer the bad luck lasts, the nearer we are to good, since nothing lasts forever."

"Bah!" she would say. "Every time you come home a fool enters the house."

"Well, well!" said he, trying to calm her, "with health and hope a man is lucky, and I have both in plenty."

One day his luck changed. There had been much talk of a certain big fish which had been seen often, and the rich man of that place offered a purse of gold to the one who would catch it. Then, wonder of wonders! what should be but that it leaped into the poor fisherman's boat. So he cleaned it, put it on a wooden dish, thrust a lemon in its mouth to make it look beautiful, and started through the forest to carry it to the rich man's house. On his way he came upon a poor man, in clothes so ragged that they could hardly hold together, sitting under a tree, groaning sadly.

"Now what ails you?" asked the good-hearted fisherman.

"What should it be but hunger?" was the answer. "I have eaten nothing for many days, and here you come with a fish big enough for three men with something left over. Luck is with you."

"That may well be," answered the fisherman, "yet my bread has not been buttered always on both sides, nor has it always fallen into the honey when I dropped it."

"If luck knocks at a man's door, he ought to share it with the luckless," grumbled the other.

"I was taking the fish to the rich man's house," the fisher explained.

"So you are one who shares his luck with the lucky and lets the hungry go famished," said the other, and groaned piteously.

"Not so," was the reply. "But I must say that some seem born to have the gold, and others to hold an empty purse, and—"

The beggar interrupted with, "Say no more. I may die famished."

"Now, friend," said the good-hearted fisher, "if you are in such a bad case, why, the fish is yours for the asking." So saying, he laid the fish at the beggar's feet.

Thereupon the ragged man stood up and clapped the fisher on the shoulder in high delight. "Never yet," said he, "did a good deed go unrewarded. This moment you shall have your wish granted. What is it?"

"Well," said the fisherman, "that is hard to decide."

"Wish in half a minute," said the other.

"There are so many things—" said the fisher.

"You have less than half a minute," warned the ragged man.

"Well, then, for the rest of today let me have everything I can wish for," said the fisherman.

"You are a clever fellow," answered the beggar. "It shall be so. But look to it that you choose well, and that you think of others. Until midnight, then, you may wish, and what you wish shall come to be."

With that the ragged man went his way carrying the fish, and the fisher turned his steps toward his cottage, busy with his thoughts. Presently he became aware that the wind was cold and the way long, so, without thinking, he said to himself, "Now I wish I was home and on my stool in front of a blazing fire, with a good supper on the table."

No sooner had he said the words than he found himself on his stool before the fire, and his wife sprawling in the corner and saying hard things to him, for she had been sitting in that very place.

"What silly jokes are these?" she asked, believing he had come in quietly and pushed her off the stool. "A pretty way to do! Did I not say that every time you come home a fool enters the house?"

"Peace, good woman," he replied, "I did but wish thoughtlessly, as the beggar warned me against, but I see that wishes may be dangerous, and I did not think of others."

So he told her the tale of the fish and the stranger, and how both of them might wish, and how the gift would end at midnight, wherefore they had better get busy and be thoughtful in their wishing. For a long time they argued, trying to decide, and at last, remembering the warning that he should consider others, the man said, "Well, there's one thing that can do no harm. I wish that every neighbor in this village had a house twice as large, with the finest of furniture and the best the world has to eat and drink."

The words were hardly spoken when a great uproar arose. The two ran to the window to look, and beheld a strange sight. Where had been neat cottages, each with its garden, were now buildings they had never seen before. Houses had spread to crowd one another. Some had grown so as to crowd trees sideways. They had elbowed one another, and were crooked, or bent, or partly tilted upwards to get room. So the people were much disturbed, and many were running about crying that the place was surely bewitched.

Those who were at supper found strange foods before them, since the fisher had wished the best that the world had, and there were foods of which they knew nothing. Some found boiled camel's meat on their dishes, some seal fat and whale meat, some turkey, some roast monkey, some Turkish sherbet, some haggis, and some found the fish on their forks and on the way to their mouths changed to meats they had never dreamed of and did not like. Tables, chairs, beds that they had used for a lifetime had vanished, and in their place were strange furnishings, silks, velvets, plush, seal skin or Eskimo furs. So every man, woman, and child was comfortless.

"Now see what you have done!" cried the woman. "Here is every one rich, with great houses when they put them in order, and we are in our old cottage, the poorest of the poor, fool that you are."

"I did but wish for the welfare of others," said the astonished fisherman, very miserably. "It begins to look as if with wishing comes grieving."

"Not with me," said his wife. "Hear this. I wish that this cottage was ten times as big, with furniture to match."

With that there came a strange groaning, and rumbling, and creaking, and cracking; and the room spread and spread, high and wide, so that it became great as a church. The man had been standing with his back to the fire, looking at his wife who sat on the stool, but suddenly found himself at a mighty scorching fire that promised to set fire to his clothes. He moved to one side in a hop, and, so doing, fell over a tree trunk a yard high and twenty feet long that had been a log for the fire. Then he heard his wife's voice screaming, and, looking up, saw her perched on the grown stool twenty feet in the air, in a state of terror lest she might fall. Above her head, on rafters sixty feet high, hung great hams the size of pigs, sausages too that would have killed a man had they fallen on him. So the fisherman had much trouble climbing the leg of the stool and teaching his wife to clamber down, for while he might have wished, he forgot. They could not reach the shelves, or see out of the window, or unlatch the door; and the bed was like a rich man's barn for bigness, while the fireplace was a fearful flaming cave near which they dared not go for the strong wind.

Then they saw the cat!

It was a monstrous creature whose head stood higher than theirs, with green glaring eyes and terrible whiskers, with a body like a tiger's, and long white teeth. And it came to both of them to remember that the cat was hungry. Across the floor crept the great beast, its eyes glaring, its tail waving fearfully from side to side. Then it crouched, ready to spring.

"Wish something!" cried the woman in great fear, clinging to her husband.

"Oh! I wish we were in the middle of the table," said he. Immediately they found themselves in the middle of a great bowl of fish stew, warm and waist deep, a sticky pond all of ten feet across. Slowly they waded to the edge, and the man helped the woman out, then climbed out himself, to find he was on what looked like a great plain, with a mighty loaf of bread, and knives and forks twice a man's length, and two mugs with rims as high as their heads. Also there was the cat on the table's edge, looking at them greedily. Full of fear they looked down at the floor, a dizzy height, then back at the cat which was creeping toward them.

Suddenly the fisher remembered his gift, not carefully or with thought, and wished they were on the mantel. So they found themselves there safe for a moment, but a moment only, for the cat gave a leap and sailed across the sixty-foot gap between the table and the mantel-shelf to land close to them. They might have wished themselves outside, or wished themselves big, or wished the cat dead; but they did not. They were too excited, and too nervous, and too fearful to think of anything except getting out of reach of the dreadful creature.

"I wish we were on the rafters," cried the man in great distress, and at once they were there, looking down in great fear at what had been their comfortable hearth, now so far away. Their clothes were wet and heavy with fish stew. They were tired. They were miserable. But they were safe from the cat in the corner where the rafters joined the wall.

Then came a new thing to distress them. From a black hole, that smelt horribly, there shone evil, red eyes. Then out of the dark reached a pincer-like pair of claws, then first one and then another long, thin, hairy leg; and out from the dark came a great spider as big as a platter. It stood a moment looking at them, swaying back and forth, then slowly advanced. With a scream the woman turned and fled along the rafter, the man following; nor did they stop though the way seemed long, until they came to a great rope, as thick as they were tall, that held one of the hams, and over which they had to climb.

"These wishes are terrible," wailed the woman, wringing her hands. "If ever things get right again I shall nevermore wish, but be satisfied with what I do."

"How can things ever be right again?" asked the man. "Everything is wrong. Our neighbors are ruined. We are undone. We shall perish if things are not right at midnight."

"With wishing comes grieving," said the woman.

"Alas! I wish we were all in a far-off land, where things are right, with our neighbors, where we could all begin again."

And that is how there came to be very contented people in Gaspé. For of a sudden, they and their neighbors found themselves in this good land where fish is plentiful, and where fields are green, and where men know that if they cannot make the thing they wish for, then they must wish for that which they themselves can do.

*By Charles J. Finger*

## MILLITINKLE

MILLITINKLE used to be just like any other donkey. She could not talk, she was not white, and she did not have pink ears with little golden bells in the tops of them. She worked hard for her master, carrying heavy loads and making long journeys. And everything he told her to do, Millitinkle did.

One time this man and his donkey were traveling up in the mountains. For days and days they had been making their way along narrow trails and over high passes. At last they got so far up in the mountains that soon they would be going down the other side. There they stopped at the foot of a cliff one night to sleep. The man put up his tent; and, as was his custom, he turned out Millitinkle to eat such grass as she could find. After doing this, he rolled up in his blanket and went to sleep.

In the night it started to snow. But the man knew nothing about it, for he was asleep. It snowed and snowed. In the morning when the man woke up he started to go out of the tent, and a lot of snow fell in on him. He thought, "I am lost. There is no hope for me now. My donkey has probably been frozen to death. And I shall not be able to move from here until the snow melts. What a fool I was to leave the donkey outside." With much trouble he pushed his way out of the tent and climbed up on a snow drift. Everywhere he looked, in every direction, he could see nothing but snow. It was so deep that it was over his head. He called to Millitinkle, but she did not come. At last he gave up, went back into the tent, and made up his mind to wait. There was nothing else he could do. But his heart was sad, and he wept over the horrible fate that had befallen his donkey.

Now, when the snow began to fall, Millitinkle was a long way from her master. She had not found much to eat near by, so she had wandered down the mountainside in search of grass. She was busy grazing when the storm started. Before she realized what a bad storm it was, the snow was already so deep that she could hardly lift one leg after the other. Fright seized her. She turned this way and that way in hopes of being able to move. She brayed for help. But the wind carried her voice down the mountain instead of toward the tent. All the time the snow was falling fast and heavy. The more the donkey struggled, the deeper in she got. Finally the snow covered her over completely and she felt nice and warm. "This is not so bad," she thought. "I'll rest for a while and then burrow along. I might as well travel under the snow as on top. It's warm, and there's no wind down here." So she rested and slept a little: and afterwards she began to kick and paw and make a tunnel for herself underneath the snow.

In this way she traveled for some distance, always down hill, for that was the easiest way to go. Behind her she left a long tunnel where the snow had been pushed aside and trampled down. On she went and on. She was thinking that soon she would get out, when the snow in front of her fell away, and she found herself in a cave. The walls were all of ice, and a dim light shone through them. The floor was ice too, very smooth and very slippery. Millitinkle looked around at herself; she was pure white. The snow had changed her color, and no amount of licking or shaking would change it back. This rather pleased her. She said to herself, "Now I'll be different from all other donkeys. None of them are as white or as beautiful as I am. My master won't know me when he sees me again." Then she started off at a trot down through the cave, wondering what she was going to find.

This cave that Millitinkle came into was the entrance to the palace of the Snow Queen. There the Snow Queen lived alone with all the snow fairies whose task it was to make the snow-flakes and scatter them during a storm. But the donkey did not know this. She trotted on and on, until she found herself at the door of a big room. The room was lit up with a wonderful white light that seemed to come from nowhere. From the ceiling hung long icicles that glittered and sparkled with every color of the rainbow. The walls were of ice, but as clear and pure as crystal. In the middle of the room was a high throne made of blocks of ice. On this sat the Snow Queen. She was all dressed in white fur, and on her head she wore what seemed to be a diamond crown. But it was really made of beautifully cut pieces of ice. When she saw Millitinkle at the door, she said, "What are you doing here? Neither man nor animal has ever found his way here before. Come in and let me see you."

Millitinkle trotted in and made a low bow before the queen. The queen, seeing what a beautiful animal the donkey was, said, "In all my life I have never seen a white donkey. You must stay with me. I will keep you and feed you well. Will you stay?"

Millitinkle brayed and tried to make herself understood. But it seemed impossible to make the queen see what she was trying to say. At last the donkey stood there in silence and looked sadly at the floor.

The queen said, "I see what's the matter. You can't talk. Eat this, and you'll be able to." She handed Millitinkle a small cake all covered with white frost. As soon as the donkey swallowed it, she was able to speak just like a human being. Then Millitinkle told the queen all about what had happened. And when the queen heard the story, she said, "I will send you back to your master. But first you must stay a month with me. I am all alone here. And I want you for a friend. You stay a month: then you can go to your master."

Millitinkle asked, "Do you think he will be all right?"

"I know he will," said the queen.

So Millitinkle agreed to stay a month with the Snow Queen. She lived in the palace and had a happy life.

During this month the donkey learned many things she had not known before. The Snow Queen took her from room to room and showed her the snow fairies at work. They were little white people with silver wings. All day they worked hard making snow-flakes. They made them in many shapes and in many sizes. When they were made, they put them in little baskets that seemed to be woven out of frozen cobwebs. Then, when the queen wished to have a storm anywhere, the fairies flew forth with their baskets and scattered the flakes in the wind. All this Millitinkle saw. Also she met some ice fairies. These were almost without color; they could hardly be seen. But they had a wonderful power. For wherever they touched water with their feet, that water turned into ice. All of these people lived in the palace. They were very happy and very busy. And they all loved their queen.

In return Millitinkle told the queen many things about the world of men. To these the Snow Queen always listened with a great deal of interest, for she had never heard about them before. She came to like the donkey more and more. And she dreaded the day when the animal would have to leave.

One night, while they were eating together at a silver table, a fairy came in and said, "I have been to the man's tent. He is very lonely. All day long he sits and sighs for his donkey. In this way he cannot live much longer."

The queen said, "He won't have to wait many days more. His time is nearly up."

Millitinkle was sad and said, "It isn't fair that I should stay from him. Hadn't I better go?"

But the queen insisted that the donkey stay, saying, "If you go now, you will be sorry; for your master could not find you in the snow. When the month is up, I'll give you something to make you more beautiful than you are now. Then you can go, and your master will have no trouble finding you."

So Millitinkle said no more. But she wondered what the queen meant by her words.

Finally the month was up, and the time came for the donkey to leave. She said to the queen, "Today I shall go away. You have been very kind to me and have treated me well. Now that I'm going, tell me what you are going to give me."

The queen said, "Come over here with me, where this red light from the icicle shines on the wall. You must do just as I tell you."

They walked over to the wall, and the queen made Millitinkle kneel down so that just her ears were shaded by the red light. Then she took a long, silvery icicle, and lightly touched the top of each ear. She said, "Now you have pink ears. Your master will be able to see you in the snow." But Millitinkle, who could not see her own ears, did not know whether the queen spoke the truth or not. "One thing more I want to do for you before you go," continued the queen. "I am going to give you a present to remember me by." And in the top of each of the donkey's ears she put a little golden bell. Then she said, "Now you can go. You are in every way the most beautiful donkey in the world. I wish you could stay with me forever."

Millitinkle thanked the queen for all she had done, saying, "I won't forget you. If I didn't have a master, I'd be glad to stay here. But I can't stay away from him any longer. Every time I think of you I'll do this." And the donkey shook her ears, and the bells went, "Tinkle, tinkle, tinkle."

So the queen and the donkey bade each other goodby, and Millitinkle went off by the same way she had come. Out through the cave she trotted and down through the tunnel she had made in the snow. There, when she came to the end, she stopped to rest.

While she rested, the sun shone on the snow above her, and the snow melted. It melted enough so that her pink ears stuck out. And when she wagged them, the bells went "Tinkle, tinkle, tinkle." Her master, who was sitting in the tent, heard this sound. He got up to look out, and he saw the pink ears. With a jump he was up and running through the snow. He thought, "What can those two pink things be? There's just a chance that they may be the ears of my donkey. Poor Millitinkle, she's frozen! That's why her ears are pink." He pushed his way on to where the donkey was. Just as he came near enough to see things clearly, Millitinkle stuck her head out of the snow and said, "Hello. Come help me!"

"Who is that?" said the man, for he could not believe that it was the donkey that spoke.

"Millitinkle," said the donkey. "Help me out, and I'll tell you how I learned to talk."

"Are you still alive?" asked the man, who was so surprised that he really did not know what he was saying.

"Of course I am," said Millitinkle. "But I'll freeze if you leave me here much longer."

Then the man dug the donkey out. And she told him about the wonderful things that had happened to her: How she got her pink ears. And why she had bells in them. And the man thought of nothing but how glad he was to have his donkey back. Together they made their way up to the tent. By the next day the snow had melted enough so that they could go on their journey. They were happy; they talked to each other; and they became the best of friends in the world.

*By Paul Fenimore Cooper*

## THE PIXIES' SCARF

ONCE UPON A TIME there was an old woman who went
out to pick whortleberries on Dartymoor. She carried
a tin can in one hand and a basket in the other, and she
meant to fill them both before she returned home.

Behind her came a little boy, her young grandson,
Dicky, who had asked her to take him with her across
the great windy moor. The old woman's eyes were on
the ground, on the low green bushes which spread in

a web for miles, but the little boy stared about him at the birds in the air, and the white clouds in the sky, and the great black tors like castles rising from the heather and grass.

"Grandmother, where does those birds come from?" he asked, but Mrs. Bundle shook her head.

"Never mind the birds, Dicky. Pick the worts. There's lots of worts here. 'Tis blue with 'em," and she stooped and gathered the little bloomy whortle-berries with her gnarled old fingers, stripping them from the bushes, and dropping them into her can with a rattle like beads falling in a box.

So Dicky turned his head from the blue sky and the flittering birds, and looked at the rounded bushes, like dark-green cushions. Dartymoor was more full of lovely things even than the sky, he thought, as he looked down. He crammed his red mouth with berries, and put a handful in his own little basket. Then he knelt down to look at the scurrying beetles and ants and the long-legged spiders which hurried about their business in the green and scarlet leaves.

Suddenly his attention was caught by a wisp of rainbow color, hanging on a twiggy branch of one of the bushes. He thought at first it was a spider's web, blue and green and gold; but when he picked it up he found it was woven silk, fine as the gossamer sacks which hang in the grasses, shimmering as the dewdrops in the grass.

"What have you got there?" asked old Mrs. Bundle, as she saw him twist the rag round his finger and hold it up to the sun.

"It's a pretty something I've found," said Dicky, going up to her and showing the scrap of silk.

"Drop it, Dicky, drop it! It's maybe something belonging to the Wee Folk."

She lowered her voice to a whisper and looked round as if she expected to see somebody coming.

"It's a pixie-scarf you've found, I reckon," she whispered. "Put it back. It doesn't do to touch their things. They don't like it."

She waited till he dropped the little scarf and then she went on gathering the berries, muttering to herself.

Dicky turned round and looked at the scarf. He couldn't bear to leave it, so he whisked it up again and slipped it in his pocket. Nobody would know, he told himself. He would take it home with him.

He wandered on, picking the ripe berries, following the little old woman, staring and whistling, forgetting the little silken scarf; but as he ruffled the bushes with stained purple hands, and drew aside the tiny leaves, he was surprised to see far more things than he had ever imagined before. Down in the soil he saw the rabbits in their holes, playing and sleeping, or curled in their smooth dwelling houses. He saw the rocks and the little streams and trickles of water flowing underground. Like a mirror was the ground and he watched the hidden life beneath it. Many things were there, deep down, a rusty dagger, a broken sword blade, and he wandered on, staring at the secrets he discovered.

"Grandmother," he called. "See here. Here's something under the grass," but the good old woman saw nothing at all except heather and whortleberries and the short sweet grass.

"Saints preserve us!" she cried, when Dicky scrabbled away the soil and brought up a broken crock of ancient coins. "How did you know they were there?" she asked.

"I seed 'em," said he.

She fingered the money and rubbed it on her torn skirt, but Dicky turned away. He didn't care about it. A new feeling had come to him, and he stood very still, listening, waiting.

The scent of the moor flowed to him, wild thyme and honey and moss in wet places. He could hear the countless bells of the purple heather ringing like merry church chimes, and the wind in the reeds sang like a harp, whilst the deep, dark bogs sighed and moaned.

"I won't touch these," said old Mrs. Bundle, and she threw the coins away into the bog, but Dicky only laughed, for he heard new music as they fell and were sucked down to the depths. The earth itself seemed to be whispering, and the stream answered back, speaking to the bog and the emerald mosses.

"Get on with your picking," scolded Mrs. Bundle. "You asked me to bring you with me a-worting, and here you are, finding queer things as ought to be hid. Whatever's took you, Dicky Bundle!"

But Dicky's eyes were wide with wonder, and he took no notice of his grandmother. Up in the trees were voices talking, two blackbirds were arguing, and he heard every word they said. A robin called: "Come here! Take no notice of those people below. Come here!" and a tom tit swung on a bough and chattered to its friend, the linnet.

More than that, he could hear the low reedy voices of the worms in the stream's banks, and understand their language as they murmured on and on with placid talk of this and that, and pushed their way among the grasses.

Then came the shrill whisper of fishes in the water, and he leaned over the peaty stream to see who was there. Flat round eyes stared back at him, and the fishes swam under a rock as his shadow fell on them. A king-fisher darted past, and Dicky heard its chuckle of glee as it dived and snatched up a weeping fish.

He would have stayed there all night, crouched on the stream's edge, hearkening to the talk of the creatures, listening to the music of the wild moorland, looking at the hidden life which was visible to his eyes, but his grandmother pulled his arm and shook him.

"Didn't you hear me? Dick Bundle! Come away home. My basket and pail are full to the brim, but you've only got a tuthree! Shame on you for a lazy good-for-nothing little boy."

Dicky was bewildered, and he followed her meekly along the road to the cottage down in Widdicombe, listening to voices all the way.

When they got home his grandmother emptied her fruit into the great brass pan, and soon there was a humming and bubbling as the jam simmered over the fire. Dicky took off his coat and hung it up behind the door, and when the scarf was away from him the little voices of the mice in the wainscot and birds in the garden ceased. The cat purred and he no longer knew what she said. The buzzing flies in the window lost their tiny excited voices; the spider in the corner was dumb.

"It's gone very quiet," said Dicky to his grandmother.

"Quiet? It's the same as usual. You go and fill the kettle and put it on ready for tea. Then wash your hands and face. No wonder you didn't find many berries. You ate 'em all."

Mrs. Bundle was indignant with her grandson, and when the two sat down to their tea, she thought of her son, Dicky's father, away in America, earning his living far from the village he loved. She must bring Dicky up to be a good boy, worthy of that father. She sighed, and looked at her grandson, and shook her head wearily. It was hard with her old bones to have to deal with a lazy young sky-gazer like Dicky.

"Now you can go out and play," she told Dicky when the meal was finished and the table cleared. "I shall make my jam ready for selling to customers, and maybe we shall get enough money to buy you a pair of shoes, for you sadly need them."

Dicky went out to Widdicombe Green and played at marbles with the other boys. Then Farmer Vinney let him take his brown mare to the stable, and Farmer Deacon asked him to catch a hen that had gone astray. So he was busy with this and that, until the moon came up over the hills and the stars shone in the night sky, and the great tors disappeared in the shadows.

Then Dicky went indoors for his supper of bread and milk. He went upstairs to the little room with a

crooked beam across the ceiling and he said his prayers and got into his wooden bed. Old Mrs. Bundle
came up to look at him and tuck in the clothes.

"Now go to sleep, Dicky. I've brought your jacket
upstairs, ready for morning. Go to sleep, and God bless
you, my dear."

But Dicky wasn't sleepy at all, and he lay with his
eyes wide open staring at the moon over the moor and
the tall tower of the church across the Green. After
a time he heard a high silvery bell-like voice, calling
and calling; as clear and fresh it was, just as if the
stars were speaking to one another.

"Dick Bundle! Dick Bundle!" cried the tiny voice.
"Give me back the scarf."

"Dick Bundle! Dick Bundle!" echoed a hundred
little voices, pealing like a chime of fairy bells, ringing like a field of harebells all swaying in the wind.

Dick sprang out of bed and looked through the window. In a rosebush in the narrow garden below, holding a glow-worm in his hands, sat a little man and
Dicky knew he was a pixie. He saw the little creature's
pointed cap, and his thin spindly legs, crossed as he
squatted among the roses, and he caught the green glint
of the pixie's eyes.

Behind were many more pixies, crowds of them,
perched on the garden wall, clambering in the flower-
beds, running across the grass, each one carrying a
glow-worm and calling "Dick Bundle" in its shrill
tinkling voice.

"Give us back the scarf," they sang.

"Come and fetch it," called Dick Bundle through

the window, and he went to his jacket pocket and took the wisp of rainbow silk and held it dangling at the window.

How beautiful it looked! It was quite different with the moon shining upon it, and it moved like a shimmering fish, and glittered in his hands.

"Oh! Oh! Oh!" sang the pixies. "There it is! There it is! Give it back!"

"Come and fetch it," said Dicky again, for he wanted to try to catch one of the little men.

"We can't come in because you said your prayers," they replied, and others echoed: "Prayers. Prayers. No, we can't come in," and their voices wailed and squeaked.

"You come down to us," invited the first pixie, who seemed to be the leader. "You bring it to us, Dick Bundle."

"No," replied Dick. "I can't do that," and he folded the scarf and drew it through his fingers. "I mustn't go out in the night, or I should catch rheumatics like my Granny."

He looked at his fingers and they were shining with light where the scarf had touched them. Yes, it was too lovely a thing to lose!

"Throw it down to us, Dicky boy," wheedled the nearest pixie. "It belongs to our Queen, and she has been hunting it all day."

"How did you know it was here?" asked Dicky. "I've never had it out of my pocket until now."

"The birds and the fishes and the rabbits all knew you heard their voices, for you stopped to listen, and no human can understand what the other world says. Only the pixies know. So when they told us a boy had hearkened to their talk as they spoke to one another, and had found old coins lost under the ground, and had bent his head to listen to the heather bells and the gossamer harps in the bushes, then we knew you must have found the scarf. For it gives eyes and ears to those who are blind and deaf."

"I'm not blind or deaf," protested Dicky.

"Yes, you are. You can see nothing without the scarf. Throw it back to us, for you can't keep it. We shall torment you till we get it."

"What will you give me for it?" asked Dicky.

"A carriage and pair," said the pixie.

"Show it to me first," said Dicky.

Then a tiny carriage rolled across the garden path, and it was made out of a cunningly carved walnut shell, drawn by a pair of field mice. The carriage was lined with green moss, and the coachman was a grasshopper with a whip of moonshine.

"I can't get into that," Dick complained. "That's no good to me."

He watched the little carriage bowl along into the shadows.

"What else will you give me?"

"A suit of armor," suggested the pixie.

"Show me first," said Dicky, and he leaned low, expecting to see a grand iron suit like the knights of old wore.

A little man staggered along the wall under the window, carrying a suit of shining armor, and the plates

were made of fishes' scales, all blue and silver, and the
helmet was adorned with a robin's feather.

"No, I couldn't wear that," said Dicky. "What else
have you got?" He twisted the little scarf and waved
it before the throng of agitated pixies, who wailed,
"Oh! Oh! Oh!" as they gazed at it and held out their
skinny arms for it.

"I'll give you a fine dress for your grandmother,"
said the pixie. He brought out of the rose tree a little
crinolined dress made of a hundred rose petals.

"My grannie's too stout for that," laughed Dicky.
"What else can you give me?"

The pixies scratched their heads with vexation. They
didn't know what to give the great human boy who
leaned from the window under the thatched roof. All
their belongings were far too small for such a giant,
they whispered to one another.

Then one of them had a thought. "A bag of marbles,"
said he.

Now Dicky was the champion marble player of
Widdicombe-on-the-Moor, and he thought if he got
some pixie marbles he might be the best player on the
whole of Dartymoor.

Surely a pixie marble would capture every other,
for there would be magic in it!

"Show them to me," said Dicky, eagerly.

The little man dragged a brown sack up the wall,
and emptied the marbles in a shining pile. Green as
grass in April, blood-red, snow-white, and blue as the
night sky they shone, each one sparkling in the moonlight.

He held out his hand for the sack, and dropped the scarf from the window, but he took care to grasp the sack before he let the scarf flutter down, for he had heard of the tricky way of pixies, who outwit humans whenever it is possible. But they were so eager to get their precious scarf, they never even snatched at the bag. With excited happy cries, queer fluting songs, and chuckles like a flock of starlings at evening, they clasped the scarf. Then singing, whistling, shouting, and waving their glow-worms, they ran away, and Dick could see the tiny lights disappear in the distance.

He put the little brown sack under his pillow, and crept into bed, for suddenly he was very tired and sleepy.

The next morning his grandmother aroused him, and he got ready for school.

"What have you got in that queer bag, Dicky?" asked Mrs. Bundle, as Dicky stuffed it in his pocket. He brought it out reluctantly and showed it to her.

"Don't throw them away, Grannie. They're pixie marbles," said Dick, frightened that he would lose his new possession.

"Pixie marbles? They are pixie rubies and emeralds and I don't know what!" cried his grandmother, holding up the glittering gems to the sunlight.

"You mustn't take them away," said Dicky, sulkily. "I am going to take them to school to play marbles."

"These will buy all of the marbles in the world, Dicky," said Mrs. Bundle. "Now we shall be rich as rich. We will build a neat little house, and have an orchard, and keep a few cows and a horse or two."

"And some pigs?" asked Dicky, quickly.

"Yes, pigs and hens and ducks, too. Yes, all of those and more besides. Perhaps we will have a donkey."

"And a new pair of boots for me and a dress for you, Grannie?" asked Dicky.

"Yes, boots and a dress and a suit of good clothes, my child. Then I will write to your father and bring him home, for we must have him to help with the farm, mustn't we?"

"Yes, oh yes," shouted Dicky, flinging his arms around her. "And we'll live on Devonshire junket and cream, shall we Grannie?"

"Maybe we will," she replied. "I think we can manage it."

She trickled the jewels through her fingers, and tried to calculate their worth. Days of poverty were over; she could sit and rest in her old age, and help others, poor as herself. Yes, the pixies had brought fortune to her cottage.

But Dicky Bundle went running off, lest he should be late for school. In his pocket was one of the gems, a smooth round blood-red stone. It made a famous marble, and never missed its aim, so that Dicky became the champion player of all the boys on Dartymoor. That was more important than riches to him, and he took care to tell nobody, where his marbles came from, lest it, too, should be sold, for money isn't everything.

*By Alison Uttley*

## ELSIE PIDDOCK SKIPS IN HER SLEEP

ELSIE PIDDOCK lived in Glynde under Caburn, where
lots of other little girls lived too. They lived mostly on
bread-and-butter because their mothers were too poor to
buy cake. As soon as Elsie began to hear, she heard the

217

other little girls skipping every evening after school in the lane outside her mother's cottage. SWISH-SWISH! went the rope through the air. TAPPITY-TAP! went the little girls' feet on the ground. MUMBLE-UMBLE-UMBLE! went the children's voices, saying a rhyme that the skipper could skip to. In course of time, Elsie not only heard the sounds, but understood what they were all about, and then the MUMBLE-UMBLE turned itself into words like this:

"ANdy
SPANdy
SUGARdy
CANdy,
FRENCH
ALmond
ROCK!
Breadandbutterforyoursupper'sallyourmother'sgot!"

The second bit went twice as fast as the first bit, and when the little girls said it, Elsie Piddock, munching her supper, always munched her mouthful of bread-and-butter in double-quick time. She wished she had some Sugardy-Candy-French-Almond-Rock to suck during the first bit, but she never had.

When Elsie Piddock was three years old, she asked her mother for a skipping-rope.

"You're too little," said her mother. "Bide a bit till you're a bigger girl, then you shall have one."

Elsie pouted and said no more. But in the middle of the night her parents were awakened by something going SLAP-SLAP! on the floor, and there was Elsie in her nightgown skipping with her father's braces. She skipped till her feet caught in the tail of them, and she tumbled down and cried. But she had skipped ten times running first.

"Bless my buttons, Mother!" said Mr. Piddock. "The child's a born skipper."

And Mrs. Piddock jumped out of bed full of pride, rubbed Elsie's elbows for her, and said: "There-a-there now! Dry your tears, and tomorrow you shall have a skip-rope all of your own."

So Elsie dried her eyes on the hem of her nightgown; and in the morning, before he went to work, Mr. Piddock got a little cord, just the right length, and made two little wooden handles to go on the ends. With this Elsie skipped all day, scarcely stopping to eat her breakfast of bread-and-butter, and her dinner of bread-and-butter. And in the evening, when the school-children were gathered in the lane, Elsie went out among them, and began to skip with the best.

"Oh!" cried Joan Challon, who was the champion skipper of them all, "just look at little Elsie Piddock skipping as never so!"

All the skippers stopped to look, and then to wonder. Elsie Piddock certainly *did* skip as never so, and they called their mothers to come and see. And the mothers in the lane came to their doors, and threw up their hands, and cried: "Little Elsie Piddock is a born skipper!"

By the time she was five she could outstrip any of them: whether in "Andy Spandy," "Lady, Lady, Drop

Your Purse," "Charley, Parley Stole Some Barley," or whichever of the games it might be. By the time she was six her name and fame were known to all the villagers in the county. And by the time she was seven, the fairies heard of her. They were very fond of skipping themselves, and they had a special Skipping-Master who taught them new skips every month at the new moon. As they skipped, they chanted:

"The High Skip,
The Sly Skip,
The Skip like a Feather,
The Long Skip,
The Strong Skip,
And the Skip All Together!

"The Slow Skip,
The Toe Skip,
The Skip Double-Double,
The Fast Skip,
The Last Skip,
And the Skip against Trouble!"

All these skips had their own meanings, and were made up by the Skipping-Master, whose name was Andy-Spandy. He was very proud of his fairies, because they skipped better than the fairies of any other county; but he was also very severe with them if they did not please him. One night he scolded Fairy Heels-o'-Lead for skipping badly, and praised Fairy Flea-Foot for skipping well. Then Fairy Heels-o'-Lead sniffed and snuffed, and said, "Hhm-hhm-hhm! There's a little girl in Glynde who could skip Flea-Foot round the moon and back again. A born skipper she is and she skips as never so."

"What is her name?" asked Andy-Spandy.

"Her name is Elsie Piddock, and she has skipped down every village from Didling to Wannock."

"Go and fetch her here!" commanded Andy-Spandy.

Off went Heels-o'-Lead, and poked her head through Elsie's little window under the eaves, crying: "Elsie Piddock! Elsie Piddock! There's a Skipping Match on Caburn, and Fairy Flea-Foot says she can skip better than you."

Elsie Piddock was fast asleep, but the words got into her dream, so she hopped out of bed with her eyes closed, took her skipping rope, and followed Heels-o'-Lead to the top of Mount Caburn, where Andy-Spandy and the fairies were waiting for them.

"Skip, Elsie Piddock!" said Andy-Spandy, "and show us what you're worth!"

Elsie twirled her rope and skipped in her sleep, and as she skipped she murmured:

"ANdy
SPANdy
SUGARdy
CANdy,
FRENCH
ALmond
ROCK!
Breadandbutterforyoursupper'sallyourmother'sgot!"

Andy-Spandy watched her skipping, with his eyes as sharp as needles, but he could find no fault with it, nor could the fairies.

"Very good, as far as it goes!" said Andy-Spandy, "Now let us see how far it *does* go. Stand forth, Elsie and Flea-Foot, for the Long Skip."

Elsie had never done the Long Skip, and if she had had all her wits about her she wouldn't have known what Andy-Spandy meant; but as she was dreaming, she understood him perfectly. So she twirled her rope, and as it came over jumped as far along the ground as she could, about twelve feet from where she had started. Then Flea-Foot did the Long Skip, and skipped clean out of sight.

"Hum!" said Andy-Spandy. "Now, Elsie Piddock, let us see you do the Strong Skip."

Once more Elsie understood what was wanted of her; she put both feet together, jumped her rope, and came down with all her strength, so that her heels sank into the ground. Then Flea-Foot did the Strong Skip, and sank in the ground as deep as her waist.

"Hum!" said Andy-Spandy. "And now, Elsie Piddock, let us see you do the Skip All Together."

At his words, all the fairies leaped to their ropes, and began skipping as lively as they could, and Elsie with them. An hour went by, two hours, and three hours; one by one the fairies fell down exhausted, and Elsie Piddock skipped on. Just before morning she was skipping all by herself.

Then Andy-Spandy wagged his head and said: "Elsie Piddock, you are a born skipper. There's no tiring you at all. And for that you shall come once a month to Caburn when the moon is new, and I will teach you to skip till a year is up. And after that I'll wager there won't be a mortal or fairy to touch you."

Andy-Spandy was as good as his word. Twelve times during the next year Elsie Piddock rose up in her sleep with the new moon, and went to the top of Mount Caburn. There she took her place among the fairies, and learned to do all the tricks of the skipping-rope, until she did them better than any. At the end of the year she did the High Skip so well that she skipped right over the moon.

In the Sly Skip, not a fairy could catch her, or know where she would skip to next; so artful was she that she could skip through the lattice of a skeleton leaf, and never break it.

She doubled the Skip Double-Double, in which you only had to double yourself up twice round the skipping-rope before it came down. Elsie Piddock did it four times.

In the Fast Skip, she skipped so fast you couldn't see her, though she stood on the same spot all the time.

In the Last Skip, when all the fairies skipped over the same rope in turn, running round and round till they made a mistake from giddiness, Elsie never got giddy, and never made a mistake, and was always left in last.

In the Slow Skip, she skipped so slow that a mole had time to throw up his hill under her rope before she came down.

In the Toe Skip, when all the others skipped on their

tip-toes, Elsie never touched a grass-blade with more than the edge of her toe-nail.

In the Skip against Trouble, she skipped so joyously that Andy-Spandy himself chuckled with delight.

In the Long Skip, she skipped from Caburn to the other end of Sussex, and had to be fetched back by the wind.

In the Strong Skip, she went right under the earth, as a diver goes under the sea, and the rabbits, whose burrow she had disturbed, handed her up again.

But in the Skip like a Feather she came down like gossamer, so that she could alight on a spider-thread and never shake the dew-drop off.

And in the Skip All Together, she could skip down the whole tribe of fairies, and remain fresh as a daisy. Nobody had ever found out how long Elsie Piddock could skip without getting tired, for everybody else got tired first. Even Andy-Spandy didn't know.

At the end of the year he said to her: "Elsie Piddock, I have taught you all. Bring me your skipping-rope, and you shall have a Prize."

Elsie gave her rope to Andy-Spandy, and he licked the two little wooden handles, first the one and then the other. When he handed the rope back to her, one of the handles was made of Sugar Candy, and the other of French Almond Rock.

"There!" said Andy-Spandy. "Though you suck them never so, they will never grow less, and you shall therefore suck sweet all your life. And as long as you are little enough to skip with this rope, you shall skip as I have taught you. But when you are too big for this rope, and must get a new one, you will no longer be able to do all the fairy skips that you have learned, although you will skip better in the mortal way than any other girl that was ever born. Good-by, Elsie Piddock."

"Aren't I ever going to skip for you again?" asked Elsie Piddock in her sleep.

But Andy-Spandy didn't answer. For morning had come over the Downs, and the fairies disappeared, and Elsie Piddock went back to bed.

If Elsie had been famous for her skipping before this fairy year, you can imagine what she became after it. She created so much wonder that she hardly dared to show all she could do. Nevertheless, for another year she did such incredible things that people came from far and near to see her skip over the church spire, or through the split oak-tree in the Lord's Park, or across the river at its widest point. When there was trouble in her mother's house or any house in the village, Elsie Piddock skipped so gaily that the trouble was forgotten in laughter. And when she skipped all the old games in Glynde, along with the little girls, and they sang:

"ANdy
SPANdy
SUGARdy
CANdy,
FRENCH
ALmond
*rock!*
Breadandbutterforyoursupper'sallyourmother'sgot!"

Elsie Piddock said: "It aren't all *I've* got!" and gave them all a suck of her new skipping-rope handles all round. And on the night of the new moon, she always led the children up Mount Caburn, where she skipped more marvelously than ever. In fact, it was Elsie Piddock who established the custom of New-Moon-Skipping on Caburn.

But at the end of another year she had grown too big to skip with her little rope. She laid it away in a box, and went on skipping with a longer one. She still skipped as never so, but her fairy tricks were laid away with the rope, and though her friends teased her to do the marvelous things she used to do, Elsie Piddock only laughed, and shook her head, and never told why. In time, when she was still the pride and wonder of the village, people would say: "Ah, but you should ha' seen her when she was a littling! Why, she could skip through her mother's key-hole!" and in more time, these stories became a legend that nobody believed. And in still more time, Elsie grew up (though never very much), and became a little woman, and gave up skipping, because skipping time was over. After fifty years or so, nobody remembered that she had ever skipped at all. Only Elsie knew. For when times were hard, and they often were, she sat by the hearth with her dry crust and no butter, and sucked the Sugar Candy that Andy-Spandy had given her for life.

It was ever and ever so long afterwards. Three new Lords had walked in the Park since the day when Elsie Piddock had skipped through the split oak. Changes

had come in the village; old families had died out, new
families had arrived; others had moved away to distant
parts, the Piddocks among them. Farms had changed
hands, cottages had been pulled down, and new ones had
been built. But Mount Caburn was as it always had
been, and as the people came to think it always would
be. And still the children kept the custom of going there
each new moon to skip. Nobody remembered how this
custom had come about, it was too far back in the years.
But customs are customs, and the child who could not
skip the new moon in on Caburn stayed at home and
cried.

Then a new Lord came to the Park; one not born a
Lord, who had grown rich in trade, and bought the old
estate. Soon after his coming, changes began to take
place more violent than the pulling down of cottages.
The new Lord began to shut up foot-paths and destroy
rights of way. He stole the Common rights here and
there, as he could. In his greed for more than he had
got, he raised rents and pressed the people harder than
they could bear. But bad as the high rents were to them,
they did not mind these so much as the loss of their old
rights. They fought the new Lord, trying to keep what
had been theirs for centuries, and sometimes they won
the fight, but oftener lost it. The constant quarrels bred
a spirit of anger between them and the Lord, and out of
hate he was prepared to do whatever he could to spite
them.

Amongst the lands over which he exercised a certain
power was Caburn. This had always been open to the
people, and the Lord determined, if he could, to close it.

Looking up the old deeds, he discovered that, though the Down was his, he was obliged to leave a way upon it by which the people could go from one village to another. For hundreds of years they had made a short cut of it over the top.

The Lord's Lawyer told him that, by the wording of the deeds, he could never stop the people from traveling by way of the Downs.

"Can't I!" snorted the Lord. "Then at least I will make them travel a long way round!"

And he had plans drawn up to inclose the whole of the top of Caburn, so that nobody could walk on it. This meant that the people must trudge miles round the base, as they passed from place to place. The Lord gave out that he needed Mount Caburn to build great factories on.

The village was up in arms to defend its rights.

"Can he do it?" they asked those who knew; and they were told: "It is not quite certain, but we fear he can." The Lord was not quite certain either, but he went on with his plans, and each new move was watched with anger and anxiety by the villagers. And not only by the villagers; for the fairies saw that their own skipping-ground was threatened. How could they ever skip there again when the grass was turned to cinders, and the new moon blackened by chimney-smoke?

The Lawyer said to the Lord: "The people will fight you tooth and nail."

"Let 'em!" blustered the Lord; and he asked uneasily: "Have they a leg to stand on?"

"Just half a leg," said the Lawyer. "It would be as well not to begin building yet, and if you can come to terms with them you'd better."

The Lord sent word to the villagers that, though he undoubtedly could do what he pleased, he would, out of his good heart, restore to them a footpath he had blocked if they would give up all pretensions to Caburn.

"Footpath, indeed!" cried stout John Maltman, among his cronies at the Inn. "What's a footpath to Caburn? Why, our mothers skipped there as children, and our children skip there now. And we hope to see our children's children skip there. If Caburn top be built over, 'twill fair break my little Ellen's heart."

"Ay, and my Margery's," said another.

"And my Mary's and Kitty's!" cried a third. Others spoke up, for nearly all had daughters whose joy it was to skip on Caburn at the new moon.

John Maltman turned to their best adviser, who had studied the matter closely, and asked: "What think ye? Have we a leg to stand on?"

"Only half a one," said the other. "I doubt if you can stop him. It might be as well to come to terms."

"None of his footpaths for us," swore stout John Maltman. "We'll fight the matter out."

So things were left for a little, and each side wondered what the next move would be. Only the people knew in their hearts that they must be beaten in the end, and the Lord was sure of his victory. So sure that he had great loads of bricks ordered; but he did not begin building for fear the people might grow violent, and perhaps burn his bricks and destroy his property. The only thing he did was to put a wire fence round the top of Caburn, and set a keeper there to send the people round it. The people broke the fence in many places, and jumped it, and crawled under it; and as the keeper could not be everywhere at once, many of them crossed the Down almost under his nose.

One evening, just before the new moon was due, Ellen Maltman went into the woods to cry. For she was the best skipper under Mount Caburn, and the thought that she would never skip there again made her more unhappy than she had ever thought she could be. While she was crying in the dark, she felt a hand on her shoulder, and a voice said to her: "Crying for trouble, my dear? That'll never do!"

The voice might have been the voice of a withered leaf, it was so light and dry; but it was also kind, so Ellen checked her sobs and said: "It's a big trouble, ma'am; there's no remedy against it *but* to cry."

"Why yes, there is," said the withered voice. "Ye should skip against trouble, my dear."

At this Ellen's sobs burst forth anew. "I'll never skip no more!" she wailed. "If I can't skip the new moon in on Caburn, I'll never skip no more."

"And why can't you skip the new moon in on Caburn?" asked the voice.

Then Ellen told her.

After a little pause the voice spoke quietly out of the darkness. "It's more than you will break their hearts, if they cannot skip on Caburn. And it must not be; it must not be. Tell me your name."

"Ellen Maltman, ma'am, and I do love skipping. I can skip down anybody, ma'am, and they say I skip as never so!"

"They do, do they?" said the withered voice. "Well, Ellen, run you home and tell them this. They are to go up to the Lord and tell him he shall have his way and build on Caburn, if he will first take down the fence and let all who have ever skipped there skip there once more by turns, at the new moon. *All*, mind you, Ellen. And when the last skipper skips the last skip, he may lay his first brick. And let it be written out on paper, and signed and sealed."

"But, ma'am!" said Ellen, wondering.

"No words, child. Do as I tell you." And the withered voice sounded so compelling that Ellen resisted no more. She ran straight to the village, and told the story to everybody.

At first they could hardly swallow it; and even when they had swallowed it, they said: "But what's the sense of it?" But Ellen persisted and persisted; something of the spirit of the old voice got into her words, and against their reason the people began to think it was the thing to do. To cut a long story short, they sent the message to the Lord next day.

The Lord could scarcely believe his ears. He rubbed his hands, and chortled at the people for fools.

"They've come to terms!" he sneered. "I shall have the Down, and keep my footpath too. Well, they shall have their Skipping Party; and the moment it is ended, up go my factories."

The paper was drawn out, signed by both parties in

the presence of witnesses, and duly sealed; and on the night of the new moon, the Lord invited a party of his friends to go with him to Caburn to see the sight.

And what a sight it was for them to see; every little girl in the village was there with her skipping-rope, from the toddlers to those who had just turned up their hair. Nay, even the grown maidens and the young mothers were there; and the very matrons, too, had come with ropes. Had they not once as children skipped on Caburn? And the message had said "All." Yes, and the others were there—others they could not see: Andy-Spandy and his fairy team, Heels-o'-Lead, Flea-Foot, and all the rest were gathered round to watch with bright fierce eyes the last great skipping on their precious ground.

The skipping began. The toddlers first, a skip or so apiece, a stumble and they fell out. The Lord and his party laughed aloud at the comical mites, and at another time the villagers would have laughed too. But there was no laughter in them tonight. Their eyes were bright and fierce like those of the fairies. After the toddlers the little girls skipped in the order of their ages, and as they got older, the skipping got better. In the thick of the school-children, "This will take some time," said the Lord impatiently. And when Ellen Maltman's turn came, and she went into her thousands, he grew restive. But even she, who could skip as never so, tired at last; her foot tripped and she fell on the ground with a little sob. None lasted even half her time; of those who followed some were better, some were worse than others; and in the small hours the older women were beginning to take their turn. Few of them kept it up for half a minute; they hopped and puffed bravely, but their skipping days were done. As they had laughed at the babies, so now the Lord's friends jibed at the babies' grandmothers.

"Soon over now," said the Lord, as the oldest of the women who had come to skip, a fat old dame of sixty-seven, stepped out and twirled her rope. Her foot caught in it; she staggered, dropped the rope, and hid her face in her hands.

"Done!" shouted the Lord; and he brandished at the crowd a trowel and a brick he had brought with him. "Clear out, the lot of you! I am going to lay the first brick. The skipping's ended!"

"No, if you please," said a gentle withered voice, "it is *my* turn now." And out of the crowd stepped a tiny tiny woman, so very old, so very bent and fragile, that she seemed to be no bigger than a little child.

"You!" cried the Lord. "Who are *you?*"

"My name is Elsie Piddock, if you please, and I am a hundred and nine years old. For the last seventy-nine years I have lived over the border, but I was born in Glynde, and I skipped on Caburn as a child." She spoke like one in a dream and her eyes were closed.

"Elsie Piddock! Elsie Piddock!" the name ran in a whisper round the crowd.

"Elsie Piddock!" murmured Ellen Maltman. "Why, mum, I thought Elsie Piddock was just a tale."

"Nay, Elsie Piddock was no tale!" said the fat woman who had skipped last. "My mother Joan skipped with her many a time, and told me tales you never would believe."

"Elsie Piddock!" they all breathed again; and a wind seemed to fly round Mount Caburn, shrilling the name with glee. But it was no wind, it was Andy-Spandy and his fairy team, for they had seen the skipping-rope in the tiny woman's hands. One of the handles was made of Sugar Candy, and the other was made of French Almond Rock.

But the new Lord had never even heard of Elsie Piddock as a story; so laughing coarsely once again, he said: "One more bump for an old woman's bones! Skip, Elsie Piddock, and show us what you're worth."

"Yes, skip Elsie Piddock," cried Andy-Spandy and the fairies, "and show them what you're worth."

Then Elsie Piddock stepped into the middle of the onlookers, twirled her baby rope over her little shrunken body, and began to skip. And she skipped as never so!

First of all she skipped:

"ANdy
SPANdy
SUGARdy
CANdy,
FRENCH
ALmond
ROCK!
Breadandbutterforyoursupper'sallyourmother'sgot!"

And nobody could find fault with her skipping. Even the Lord gasped: "Wonderful! Wonderful for an old woman!" But Ellen Maltman, who *knew,* whispered: "Oh, mum! 'tis wonderful for *any*body! And oh, mum, do but see—she's skipping in her sleep!"

It was true. Elsie Piddock, shrunk to the size of seven years old, was sound asleep, skipping the new moon in with her baby rope that was up to all the tricks. An hour went by, two hours, three hours. There was no stopping her, and no tiring her. The people gasped, the Lord fumed, and the fairies turned head-over-heels for joy. When morning broke the Lord cried: "That's enough!"

But Elsie Piddock went on skipping.

"Time's up!" cried the Lord.

"When I skip my last skip, you shall lay your first brick," said Elsie Piddock.

The villagers broke out into a cheer.

"Signed and sealed, my Lord; signed and sealed," said Elsie Piddock.

"But hang it, old woman, you can't go on forever!" cried the Lord.

"Oh, yes, I can," said Elsie Piddock. And on she went.

At midday the Lord shouted: "Will the woman never stop?"

"No, she won't," said Elsie Piddock. And she didn't.

"Then I'll stop you!" stormed the Lord, and made a grab at her.

"Now for a Sly Skip," said Elsie Piddock, and skipped right through his thumb and forefinger.

"Hold her, you!" yelled the Lord to his Lawyer.

"Now for a High Skip," said Elsie Piddock, and as

the Lawyer darted at her, she skipped right over the highest lark singing in the sun.

The villagers shouted for glee, and the Lord and his friends were furious. Forgotten was the compact signed and sealed—their one thought now was to seize the maddening old woman, and stop her skipping by sheer force. But they couldn't. She played all her tricks on them: High Skip, Slow Skip, Sly Skip, Toe Skip, Long Skip, Fast Skip, Strong Skip, but never Last Skip. On and on and on she went. When the sun began to set, she was still skipping.

"Can we never rid the Down of the old thing?" cried the Lord desperately.

"No," answered Elsie Piddock in her sleep, "the Down will never be rid of me more. It's the children of Glynde I'm skipping for, to hold the Down for them and theirs forever; it's Andy-Spandy I'm skipping for once again, for through him I've sucked sweet all my life. Oh, Andy, even you never knew how long Elsie Piddock could go on skipping!"

"The woman's mad!" cried the Lord. "Signed and sealed doesn't hold with a madwoman. Skip or no skip, I shall lay the first brick!"

He plunged his trowel into the ground, and forced his brick down into the hole as a token of his possession of the land.

"Now," said Elsie Piddock, "for a Strong Skip!"

Right on the top of the brick she skipped, and down underground she sank out of sight, bearing the brick beneath her. Wild with rage, the Lord dived after her. Up came Elsie Piddock skipping blither than ever—but the Lord never came up again. The Lawyer ran to look down the hole; but there was no sign of him. The Lawyer reached his arm down the hole; but there was no reaching him. The Lawyer dropped a pebble down the hole; and no one heard it fall. So strong had Elsie Piddock skipped the Strong Skip.

The Lawyer shrugged his shoulders, and he and the Lord's friends left Mount Caburn for good and all. Oh, how joyously Elsie Piddock skipped then!

"Skip Against Trouble!" cried she, and skipped so that everyone present burst into happy laughter. To the tune of it she skipped the Long Skip, way out of sight. And the people went home to tea. Caburn was saved for their children and for the fairies, forever.

But that wasn't the end of Elsie Piddock; she has never stopped skipping on Caburn since, for Signed and Sealed is Signed and Sealed. Not many have seen her, because she knows all the tricks; but if you go to Caburn at the new moon, you may catch a glimpse of a tiny bent figure, no bigger than a child, skipping all by itself in its sleep, and hear a gay little voice, like the voice of a dancing yellow leaf, singing:

"ANdy
SPANdy
SUGARdy
CANdy,
FRENCH
ALmond
*rock!*

Breadandbutterforyoursupper'sallyourmother'sgot!"

*By Eleanor Farjeon*

# TOLD
# UNDER THE
# MAGIC UMBRELLA

*Compiled by the Literature Committee*

*of the*

## ASSOCIATION FOR CHILDHOOD EDUCATION

DOROTHY W. BARUCH, *Whittier College*

JEAN BETZNER, *Teachers College, Columbia University*

FRANCES KERN, *National College of Education*

ANNIE E. MOORE

ELOISE RAMSEY, *Wayne University*

KATHERINE REEVES, *New York State College of Home Economics, Cornell University*

MARTHA SEELING, *Roslyn Heights Public Schools*

MARY REED WOOD, *Trenton Public Schools*

MARY LINCOLN MORSE, *Chairman*

# A MESSAGE TO GROWN-UPS BY WAY OF EXPLANATION

*Told Under the Magic Umbrella* has been compiled by the members of the Literature Committee of the Association for Childhood Education as a fourth volume in the series of umbrella books for young children. Its companion volumes are *Told Under the Green Umbrella,* a collection of folk and fairy tales; *Told Under the Blue Umbrella,* a compilation of stories, real and nearly real; and *Sung Under the Silver Umbrella,* an anthology of verse. To supplement the previous umbrella books, and with them to cover the complete field of the literary needs of children, *Told Under the Magic Umbrella* specializes in stories that are both modern and fanciful.

As members of the Literature Committee, we set no limitations to the period covered by the word "modern," yet we found many more than a majority of the stories we had selected as childlike, and for both story and fancy, written in the near-by present and in the language of present-day life. This seems an evidence of the growing art in story writing for the children of today. Surely some of the stories we have chosen will, in the future, take their places among the lasting tales of yesterday.

Our Committee, at long distance, carried on an interpretative discussion. We tried to analyze back of our stories what we believed fancy to be. Broadly

240

speaking, it was taken to mean any departure from conceded reality out into the realm of the unreal. In its simplest form it endowed characters not possessing it with the power of speech. Here a hen may talk, yet otherwise remain thoroughly henlike in character. Or again, we thought of fancy as giving to story characters the ability to act not in keeping with their own acts but with those of human beings—as when a hen markets, cooks, lives like a human being. Still further, departure from the factual was taken to involve the supernatural or superhuman or for characters and events to transcend all reality. Such tales involve fairies, witches, ogres, transformations, charms and the like. Out of this analysis we evolved a definition which we look back on (as has many another such working group as ours) with dissatisfaction. Our definition was bare bones but no more; there was no song of a nightingale in it. We leave any further defining of what we believe fantasy is, to our stories—to them and to Mrs. Bianco's Foreword.

That the field of fancy is as wide as it is varied, and is limited only by the capacity for such in human beings, was evidenced even by the differing personal reactions of our committee members to our included stories. Some of us did or did not like definite tales; but, we added, children like them—or some of them at least. On the whole, the range of stories in *Told Under the Magic Umbrella* should, we think, possess the human variety sought by and satisfying to children of divergent tastes. We regret that some of our unanimously selected stories were not available for use:

Wanda Gag's "Millions of Cats" and Hugh Lofting's "The Story of Mrs. Tubbs" are representative of such.

The stories secured for use in *Told Under the Magic Umbrella* have been arranged from the simpler ones on. Though many of them seem to reach most securely into the imaginative interests of children in the second, third and fourth grades, there are some for younger children. They suggest use with a child wherever their story and fancy fit.

No story, as story, or invested with fancy as such, not receiving a majority vote has found its way into *Told Under the Magic Umbrella.* By majority choice also, our essayist, Margery Williams Bianco, was chosen; our illustrator, Elizabeth Orton Jones, selected; and our dedication—"To the Children Who Love Wonder, Magic, Fun"—adopted. This says what we unanimously want it to say—to wonder, magic, fun our magic umbrella is consecrated. We chose our book title and agreed that its cover carry the magic color red.

In another section devoted to acknowledgments, the committee registers its appreciation to the many publishers who released for our use stories held by them. For stories suggested by other than committee members, for the editorial service of association members, and for the original publication privilege of stories generously contributed, the committee records its gratitude.

No explanation as to how *Told Under the Magic Umbrella* took its present shape would be complete without a tribute to the steady cooperation of Doris S. Patee, Children's Book Editor of our publisher, The

Macmillan Company. Miss Patee has served as adviser to each step in the preparation of our fourth umbrella. For its attractive format she alone is responsible.

In conclusion it is the hope of the members of the Literature Committee of the Association for Childhood Education that, assisted by Mrs. Bianco's foreword and the illustrative art of Miss Jones, the stories in our magic umbrella may carry children's imaginations out beyond the land of conceded reality into the realm of a joyous and spirited fancy. Here unaccountable things happen—a bear may whisper of a mother's birthday present in a little boy's ear, or, on Caburn one may catch, at the new moon, a glimpse of a tiny bent figure, no bigger than a child, skipping all by itself in its sleep. One may even hear a gay little voice, like the voice of a dancing leaf, singing:

> "ANdy
> SPANdy
> SUGARdy
> CANdy,
> FRENCH
> ALmond
> ROCK!
> Breadandbutterforyoursupper'sallyourmother'sgot!"

MARY LINCOLN MORSE, *Chairman*

# ACKNOWLEDGMENTS

FOR permission to reprint the stories included in *Told Under the Magic Umbrella* the Literature Committee of the Association for Childhood Education records its appreciation to the following:

D. Appleton-Century Company, Inc., New York, for "The Ogre That Played Jackstraws," from *The Book of Knight and Barbara* by David Starr Jordan.

Dodd, Mead & Company, Inc., New York, for "Sojo," by Erick Berry, and "The Lost Merbaby," by Mary and Margaret Baker (Copyright, 1927, by Dodd, Mead & Company, Inc.).

Doubleday, Doran & Company, Inc., New York, for "The Saddler's Horse," from *A Street of Little Shops* by Margery Williams Bianco (Copyright, 1932, by Margery Williams Bianco. Permission of Doubleday, Doran & Company, Inc.); "The Bojabi Tree," by Edith Rickert (Copyright, 1923, by Doubleday, Doran & Company, Inc.); "The Lamb That Went to Fairyland," from *The Rainbow Cat* by Rose Fyleman (Copyright, 1923, by Doubleday, Doran & Company, Inc.); "The Bean Boy," from *California Fairy Tales* by Monica Shannon (Copyright, 1926, by Doubleday, Doran & Company, Inc.).

E. P. Dutton & Company, Inc., New York, for "The Merry-Go-Round and the Griggses," from *A Merry-Go-Round of Modern Tales* by Caroline D. Emerson.

Faber & Faber, Ltd., London, for "The Three

Apples," from *Michael of Ireland* by Anne Casserley (Permission Harper & Brothers) ; "The Pixies' Scarf," from *Mustard, Pepper and Salt* by Alison Uttley.

Harcourt, Brace & Company, Inc., New York, for "How to Tell the Corn Fairies," from *Rootabaga Stories* by Carl Sandburg (Copyright, 1922, by Harcourt, Brace & Company, Inc.) ; "Rocking-Horse Land," from *Moonshine and Clover* by Laurence Housman.

Harper & Brothers, New York, for "Gooseberry Garden," by Lois Lenski; "Living in W'ales," from *The Spider's Palace* by Richard Hughes.

The Harter Publishing Company, Cleveland, for "Sojo," by Erick Berry.

J. B. Lippincott Company, Philadelphia, for "Gissing and the Telephone," from *I Know a Secret* by Christopher Morley.

Little, Brown & Company, Boston, for "The Brownie in the House," from *Seven Peas in a Pod* by Margery Bailey.

Longmans, Green & Company, New York, for "The Musical Box," by Clare Leighton.

Lothrop, Lee & Shepard Company, New York, for "Little Dog and Big Dog," by Maude Lindsay, from *A Story Garden for Little Children.*

The Macmillan Company, New York, for "Ask Mr. Bear," by Marjorie Flack.

Methodist Book Concern, Cincinnati, for "Two Little Shoes," by Carol Ryrie Brink, in *Picture Story Paper.*

William Morrow & Company, Inc., New York, for

"Millitinkle," from *Tal, His Marvelous Adventures with Noom-Zor-Noom* by Paul Fenimore Cooper.

John Murray, London, for "George and Angela," by Cicely Englefield.

Thomas Nelson & Sons, New York, for "The Little Old Woman and How She Kept Her Geese Warm," from *The Little Old Woman Who Used Her Head* by Hope Newell.

Oxford University Press, New York, for "The Cobbler's Tale," from *Ragman of Paris* by Elizabeth Orton Jones.

Frederick A. Stokes Company, New York, for "The Pony Tree," by Charlotte Brate (Copyright, 1928, by Frederick A. Stokes Company); "The Three Elevators," from *The Lively City O' Ligg* (Copyright, 1899, by Gelett Burgess); "Elsie Piddock Skips in Her Sleep," from *Martin Pippin in the Daisy Field* by Eleanor Farjeon (Copyright, 1937, by Eleanor Farjeon).

The John C. Winston Company, Philadelphia, for "If You Had a Wish?", by Charles J. Finger.

Erick Berry and *Child Life,* Chicago, for "Sojo."

Carol Ryrie Brink, for "Two Little Shoes."

Emma L. Brock, for "Gingham Lena."

Frances Anne Brown, for "A Happy Christmas Tree."

Alice Crew Gall and Fleming Crew, for "The Song of the Little Donkey."

Louise M. La Fleur and *Child Life,* Chicago, for "Little Duckling Tries His Voice," by Marjorie La Fleur.

Julian Street, for "The Goldfish" (Copyright, 1911, by the Ridgway Company; Copyright, 1912, by Dodd, Mead & Co., Inc.).

The Literature Committee acknowledges its appreciation also to May Hill Arbuthnot, Lula E. Wright, Carol Ryrie Brink, Edwina Fallis, Jennie Milton and Laura M. White for cooperative editorial service, story suggestions and other assistance to the new umbrella book.